BOOK 4

HIGH SIERRA ADVENTURE

S · E · R · I · E · S

Mountaintop Rescue

Jeff Nesbit

OLIVER
NELSON

THOMAS NELSON PUBLISHERS
Nashville · Atlanta · London · Vancouver

Published in Nashville, Tennessee, by Thomas Nelson, Inc., Publishers, and distributed in Canada by Word Communications, Ltd., Richmond, British Columbia.

Library of Congress Cataloging-in-Publication Data

Nesbit, Jeffrey Asher.
    Mountaintop rescue / Jeff Nesbit.
        p.   cm. — (High Sierra adventure series ; bk. 4)
    Summary: While on a climbing trip with his stepfather, Josh Landis decides that he must try to rescue two young eagles from their almost inaccessible mountaintop eyrie.
    ISBN 0-8407-9257-3 (pbk.)
    [1. Sierra Nevada (Calif. and Nev.)—Fiction.
2. Eagles—Fiction. 3. Stepfathers—Fiction.
4. Christian life—Fiction.] I. Title. II. Series: Nesbit, Jeffrey Asher. High Sierra adventure series ; bk. 4.
PZ7.N4378Mo   1994
[Fic]—dc20   93-49796
                                                                         CIP
                                                                          AC

Printed in the United States of America.

1   2   3   4   5   6   —   99   98   97   96   95   94

To Joshua, whose love of animals is the inspiration and strength of these books.

Books in the High Sierra Adventure Series

△
CHAPTER 1

△ I knew there was no way the rabbit would ever escape, not out in the open like that. It should never have broken clear of its warren. It shouldn't have taken the risk.

The eagle came hurtling out of the sky at a hundred miles an hour, it seemed. Its wings were tucked in tight, its hooked beak jutting forward. Its body was streamlined perfectly for speed.

The rabbit was still a good fifty yards from anything when the eagle came to earth. The eagle spread its wings, almost like it was doing the backstroke in the air. There was a flurry of feathers in all directions.

The rabbit made one last desperate effort to change direction. But there wasn't enough time. Not now. The eagle was upon it.

In one fell swoop, the eagle clutched the rabbit in its powerful talons and began the long, slow climb back to the heavens. The rabbit's fate was sealed. The daily ritual of hunter and hunted I'd grown so accustomed to had played out once again.

"Dumb rabbit," I muttered. "Shoulda stayed put."

I watched the eagle climb higher and higher into the sky before it finally disappeared into the treeline to the east of the small outcropping where I was standing.

I'd just spent the better part of the afternoon climbing this small cliff. I was learning how to rock-climb, and my stepdad had let me practice here, alone, as long as I was careful.

It wasn't all that dangerous climbing here. Even if all of my pitons came loose and I fell from the top, it was still less than thirty feet. It was a good place to practice though, because there were lots of outcroppings. And you had a great view of the valley.

In a couple of weeks, I was going to climb a real mountain with my stepdad and my instructor, Ruth Sylvan. We were going to climb Cascade Mountain, on the western slope, about five or six miles from here.

Actually, as I watched, I realized that was probably where that eagle was now headed. The rangers had said there was a nest of golden eagles up near the peak somewhere, and that the babies were about to leave the nest and hunt on their own.

It was weird how my life had changed over the summer. Since my stepfather, my mom, and I had moved out to the Sierra Nevadas from Washington, D.C., I'd almost forgotten what it had been like to live in the suburbs.

Here, at the edge of the wilderness, I spent my days climbing rocks or wandering among huge, towering pines, or following tracks of foxes and deer for fun, or just kicking through clear, sparkling streams. I was different now.

The eagle let out one last call, proclaiming to the world that—on this day, at least—it had won. *"Screee!"* it called out, the sound coming back to me.

You could hear the eagle from a long way off—when it wanted to be heard. Its call was so distinctive. It soared so high above the earth, the sound of its loud call echoed for miles through the cathedral canyons of the High Sierras.

There is no other creature like the eagle, really. Its wingspan is immense, its grace in the air like that of an expert ballerina, and its knowledge of the wilderness landscape awesome.

An Indian legend says that when an eagle befriends you, it does so for life, that you can always count on it to come to your side in a time of trouble. I had no idea if that was true, of course.

I'd never seen an eagle close up for any length of time—other than at the National Zoo in Washington, D.C. But you can't really *see* an eagle in the zoo. Eagles belong in the sky, or in their eyries at the top of a lofty mountain.

"Screee!!!" came the sound again. I jerked my head up and scanned the sky. Something was going on, something different. The eagle had hunted. So why was it calling out? Why was it making such a ruckus?

The *crack* of the rifle shot made me jump. Rock shards tumbled down the side of the small cliff I was on. There was a second *crack*, then a third. Someone was hunting something. But what could it be?

I stared up at the sky. Off in the distance, I spotted what had to be a second eagle ripping across the sky,

3

its wings full out, its curved beak pointed down. It was almost a blur as it raced across the sea of tall pines on the steep mountain slope.

That eagle was in a hurry. This was no leisurely stroll across the sky on a lazy August afternoon. It was headed somewhere very, very fast.

Once, I'd mistaken hawks and vultures for the eagle. No more. The eagle was so distinct, so different from other birds, that, now that I knew what to look for, there was no mistaking it.

It took just several seconds for the eagle to go from the treeline to the west until it vanished behind the trees to the east of me. I'd never seen a bird move so fast.

More rifle shots broke the stillness. Only then did it dawn on me why someone was shooting with a rifle, which could send a bullet hurtling a long way with deadly accuracy.

It was because they were sighting something a long way off, something that rarely came down close to the earth. Like an eagle.

"Leave it alone," I mumbled. "It isn't hurting anything."

There was no good reason to hunt an eagle. They almost never killed cattle or sheep, like an old cougar would. They never went on rampages and threatened people in the parks, like a crazy bear will do every so often. They didn't hunt in packs, like wolves will.

No, there was only one reason to hunt an eagle. For sport. Because it looked cool when it was stuffed and sitting in someone's den. To my mind, that wasn't exactly a world-class reason to go hunt down and kill one of God's creatures.

The eagle called out again. When I didn't hear any more rifle shots, I breathed easier. So the eagle had won. This time. Next time might be different, though. There was now a new game of hunter and the hunted.

△
CHAPTER 2

△ I climbed back down the small cliff face and worked my way to a stream at the bottom that would eventually take me to my home in Ganymede.

Ganymede wasn't the name of a town, really. It was just what we called our little community of homes on the side of a very small mountain at the edge of the Sierra wilderness. We were a little outpost a few miles from Jupiter, the only town in the area. Because Ganymede is a satellite moon of the planet Jupiter, we called our little community Ganymede.

As I followed the creek back home to my house, I decided to ask my stepfather about the eagle. I was curious. Usually, an eagle will just climb higher into the sky if a hunter is nearby.

The one I'd seen was dangerously close to the treeline, where a hunter could get a decent shot at it. Why?

Before Mom and I had moved to California, I'd dreamed of the eagle. The eagle had carried me away from the side of a cliff, and I'd never forgotten the dream.

Then, soon after I'd gotten here, I'd crossed paths with a grizzly bear out in the wilderness, and an eagle had shown up briefly to hunt as well.

The grizzly hadn't attacked me, and the eagle hadn't either. But I'd been too terrified of the bear to pay much attention to the eagle, other than to notice that it hadn't gone after me, too.

Now, as I walked along the creek, kicking stones into the water, I wondered where the eagle's eyrie was. I figured my stepdad was right, that it had to be on Cascade Mountain, which was the highest peak directly to the east of our little community.

They were golden eagles, not bald eagles. My stepdad said the park service kept a lookout for the bald eagle—the symbol of our country—but there weren't any near us, really.

Bald eagles were endangered animals. They'd been hunted so often that there were only a few thousand left alive by now. Thanks to efforts by people just like my stepdad—who was a National Park Service ranger—the bald eagle population is growing.

The bald eagle isn't really bald, of course. It has a white head, and I guess people felt like it looked bald compared to its cousin, the golden eagle. Full-size, they're about three feet, but their wingspan is about seven feet or so.

Once, I spotted one circling above me when we drove near the coast, and I stared for all I was worth. They were twice the size of any bird I'd ever seen before coming to California.

At one time, the bald eagle ruled along the coast of California, Oregon, and Washington. They were sea eagles. They hunted for fish in the rivers that fed into the ocean.

But as they were hunted, they began to retreat to the highest, most inaccessible parts of the land they could find. They wanted to get away from people. That was their only hope.

The eagle atop Cascade Mountain, though, wasn't a bald eagle. It was a golden eagle, which was every bit as rare in the United States. The golden eagle mostly stayed up in Canada.

Golden eagles hunted in the wilderness of the Sierra Nevadas. They hunted most anything they could track down. A golden eagle could take down a full-grown deer if it had to, though it usually hunted smaller prey it could carry off to its mountaintop home.

As I walked along, I noticed—almost without thinking—all the different tracks that ran alongside the creek. I could recognize tracks now in my sleep. I could glance down at one and tell right off what it belonged to.

There was a skunk track off to my right—five toes, with short claws at the end, and a double footpad that was different from any other creature.

Tracks are a little like fingerprints. Every animal has a different track. Once you know what you are looking for, it is easy to tell them apart.

An otter's track, for instance, is so different from a skunk's it isn't even funny! An otter has five toes, just like the skunk, but its footpad has four hard spikes in it. It's an unmistakable track.

I thought about the eagle again. It sure couldn't spot an animal from its tracks on the earth, like I could. I

9

wondered how an eagle knew what it was hunting. Did it see the animal from the sky? Could it tell what kind it was from a mile up in the air?

The sky was beginning to grow dark to the east as I neared our house. The summer was quickly drawing to a close. The nights were starting to get a chill to them. School would start soon.

My first summer in the High Sierras had been a wild one. I'd come face to face with a grizzly, maybe the last one in this part of the country. I'd tracked a cougar that had been killing sheep. I'd survived a fight with a pack of half-breed wolves.

It was funny how I'd nearly forgotten what it was like to live in the city. It seemed ages ago. I no longer bugged my mom about whether I could get ice cream sandwiches at the store, or whether she was going to buy me the latest arcade game.

They have this new thing, a "virtual reality" game that is almost like being there. You can sit and stare at your game, press the toggle switch, and it's almost like you are right there, clinging to the precipice as you swing out over a chasm.

I laughed out loud. It seemed so funny to me. I didn't need a "virtual reality" game, something that was *almost* real. I had the real thing.

Ruth, who had taught me how to climb rocks, had taken me out over that kind of chasm. I'd clung to those precipices. I didn't have to sit in front of a computer or a TV. I'd held on to those jagged rocks with my own two hands.

In fact, Ruth would know if the eagles were on Cascade Mountain and if we'd find them when we climbed there soon. I'd ask her first thing in the morning.

△

CHAPTER 3

△ "You're sure?" Ruth asked me. She paused at the bottom of the practice cliff a few miles from our home, where she was trying to teach me how to climb solo carefully.

"Yep, I'm sure," I answered solemnly, trying to make sure my eyes didn't waver as I stared back at her.

Ruth had this way of looking at you, like she was trying to read your soul. She had this uncanny ability to look at you for the longest time without blinking, her deep-set brown eyes boring into yours. She was doing that now.

"There were rifle shots?"

"A whole bunch of 'em."

"And they were aimed at the eagles?"

"Had to be," I answered. "There was the one eagle that caught the rabbit, and then there was a second

11

that went racing toward the place where the shots came from."

"And it was in the direction of Cascade Mountain?"

"Yeah, pretty much."

Ruth pursed her lips and placed her rough, callused hands on her hips. Ruth wasn't like any woman I'd ever met before. Muscles rippled and bulged on her arms. The calves on her legs were much bigger than mine, her waist smaller.

Ruth had been a serious rock-climber for a long time. It was her passion. She spent every waking minute on the rocks. She'd climbed rock faces all over the world. She had zillions of pictures from all those trips.

I'd asked her once why she spent so much time climbing rocks. She hadn't answered me right away. Then she'd asked me a question.

"What do you do when you're on your bike and there's a tree down in the road?" she'd asked.

"I go around it," I'd answered.

"OK, so how about when you're walking along and there's a big puddle on the sidewalk?"

"Same. Go around," I'd said.

Ruth had smiled broadly. "Hmmm. But when you were very young, didn't you try to jump the tree with your bike, and didn't you stomp through the puddle, just for fun?"

"Yeah, I guess." I'd shrugged.

"Well, that's what I'm doing," she'd said. "Instead of taking the easy way around the mountain, I'm going up and over it."

I thought about that conversation now as I looked back at Ruth. She'd go right after this thing with the eagles, I knew. She wouldn't sit still for it. She

12

wouldn't take the easy way by going around the puddle. She'd stomp right through it.

My stepfather said Ruth was one of those unique people you hear about every so often. She was a devoted, outspoken Christian who told you why she believed in what she believed, but who was also really into protecting the environment.

My stepdad said the world told you that you couldn't do both. People had started thinking you had to almost worship nature and be devoted to it to show that you cared. That didn't leave much room for being devoted to God.

Ruth was trying to do both—care for nature as well as serve God—with everything she could muster. She was always talking about how it was her *duty* to protect the environment, to do what she could to help God's creation.

I liked listening to Ruth talk about those things. I guess I was coming to the same conclusions. I listened to sermons in church with my family every Sunday. They made sense to me.

It also made sense to me that nature was a perfect reflection of God's intention for the world.

The very first chapter of Genesis in the Bible talked about how God created the world. He created each of the animals and then said that it was our job to take care of them.

That was the way Ruth saw it. It was her *job*. Not like it was my stepdad's job as a National Park Service ranger, but more like her job for life: She was supposed to take care of God's creation.

"They can't go after those eagles," she said grimly.

"I think they are, though."

"What's your dad say about it?"

I didn't answer right away. People who saw me with Mark, my stepfather, just assumed he was my father. Sometimes I corrected them. More and more, though, I didn't. Like now.

"Oh, he says there isn't much we can do about it."

"But it's illegal to hunt those golden eagles, isn't it?"

"Yeah, sure. But Mark says it's like looking for a needle in a haystack."

"How so?"

"He says that because the eagles roam so far over the whole area, the hunters can wait for them almost anywhere. Shoot, it's almost ten miles in either direction, and the eagles will fly out that far."

Ruth nodded. It made sense to her. "But can't they keep track of the hunters who might be going out?"

"No way. There are too many people who just hike out there without telling anyone. Any one of them could be going after those eagles."

Ruth sighed. I could see that she wanted to do something. But she hadn't figured what just yet.

"Hm," she grunted. She tugged on the rope to make sure it was secure, planted her foot on a rock outcropping, and began to climb up hand over hand. "I'm gonna have to think about this."

"Let me know," I said. "I wanna help."

"I will," she promised. "You can count on it."

△
CHAPTER 4

△ Eagles, it turned out, will build a huge nest out of grass and all kinds of other junk way up at the top of a mountain. The same nest will stay there for years. The eagles just keep coming back to the nest, year after year.

They almost always have just one or two eggs in the spring. The babies will stay with their parents, learning how to survive, for almost a year. Then they're on their own.

Unfortunately, the old-timers told me, no one had seen any baby eagles flying for a long, long time. Not around these parts.

When I asked the rangers about this, they told me it was true, that the eagles in the area hadn't been able to raise babies successfully for the longest time.

Apparently, for some reason their eggs weren't making it. Their shells were too fragile and they were cracking before birth. There hadn't been any baby eagle births out in the wild near Jupiter and Ganymede for years.

Until this year. Hikers had told the rangers they'd seen one, maybe two baby eagles out with their parents over the summer. The babies weren't nearly ready to go out on their own, not by a long shot.

You could tell they were babies because they flew close to their mother. Plus, they were smaller in size, the hikers had told the rangers.

The babies didn't venture out much. Mostly, they hung out around the nest. They probably wouldn't be ready to go out on their own until the following spring, the rangers said.

Ruth and others were really excited about this. It was also one of the reasons why she was ready for war when I'd told her about the hunters laying in wait for the eagles.

What really amazed me was how long an eagle can live. Golden eagles have sometimes lived eighty years —as long as they aren't hunted down or killed by pesticides.

Once I started asking around, people in the town of Jupiter told me they'd seen the same eagles around the Cascade Mountain range for years.

Which meant that if hunters wanted to find them, they could. Their range was far and wide, but their home wasn't hard to find. It wasn't like they hid it from the world.

Getting to that home, though, was no easy task. Eagles usually found the highest, scariest, most inaccessible place they could possibly manage to build their eyrie.

An eyrie was almost always up above the snowline, on a crag overlooking the whole world. You couldn't get to it unless you risked your life, practically. That's why people usually left their nests alone.

But a hunter who was determined to find an eagle could camp out in the valleys below and look for them. That's what I figured I'd seen and heard the other day.

It made me so mad I couldn't see straight. I'm not sure why, really. It just didn't seem right. It didn't seem fair.

You couldn't really kill an eagle for food. There was only one reason to try to take one. You wanted to tell your friends you'd killed an eagle. I guess they thought it was like a sport to hang out in valleys and fire up at the sky.

Mark said they'd never kill them, most likely. Eagles usually flew so high up that they were well out of range from most rifles.

Even high-powered rifles with scopes? I'd asked him.

Well, if someone was well-equipped—and just bound and determined to kill an eagle—then they could probably sight and kill one from a long way off, he'd said.

Two nights running I had nightmares about hunters in valleys with long rifles and elaborate scopes on top of them, waiting for eagles to circle high on rising air currents. There would be the sharp *crack!* of a rifle shot. Then a bird would come plummeting to the earth.

Mark promised me the rangers would keep an extra lookout for people within twenty miles or so of the Cascade Mountain range, but there wasn't anything you could do about it, really. He couldn't promise me

17

they'd find anything, he'd said. It was just too difficult.

I wished with all my heart there was some way we could warn the eagles, maybe climb up to their eyrie and tell them just to stay put for a while until the hunters got bored.

But that was crazy. Mark and Ruth both said it was pretty much impossible to get to the eyrie. It was crazy to even think about trying. And even if you got there, there was nothing you could do. The eagles wouldn't understand.

I still wanted to try. I kept asking Ruth about how she'd get to the eyrie, what she would do. She kept telling me to forget about it.

But I couldn't forget about it. I just couldn't. It stayed with me, night and day. I don't know why. I couldn't get that picture of the soaring eagle out of my mind.

I wanted to get to that eyrie, somehow, some way. I just had this feeling that I could help. It was crazy, I know. But I couldn't get rid of the thought, no matter how hard I tried.

$\triangle$

CHAPTER 5

$\triangle$ "You're totally out of your mind," Ashley said.

I grinned from ear to ear. "I know."

Ashley—my best friend who lives right around the corner from our log home in the little community of Ganymede—was being her usual pain. She questioned everything I ever did or said.

The sky was blue, I'd say. Nope, mostly white, because of the clouds, she'd answer.

She was doing it again. She said I'd lost my mind over these stupid eagles.

"Forget about it," she said, shaking her head. "There's nothing you can do about it. Absolutely nothing. It's a lost cause."

"But what if I can get up there?"

"To their nest, their . . . what do you call it?"

"Eyrie."

"Yeah, that. Even if you get there—which you can't,

19

you know, because it's like totally impossible—but even if you could, what would you do then?"

"I dunno." I shrugged. "Something. Tell them to watch out for the hunters."

Ashley groaned with total disgust. "You can't *tell* an eagle to watch out. Are you crazy?"

"Maybe."

"Maybe totally," Ashley said.

We were hanging out, involved in our favorite game. Both of us had become pretty good trackers over the course of the summer. Sometimes we'd go out in the morning, try to pick up the most unusual track we could find along the creek bottom, and track it back to its source to see what was up.

We'd run across some pretty unusual things. Once, we ran smack into a bobcat. Another time we found a skunk and got sprayed. Ashley caught more than I did, and the odor had hung around her for a couple of days.

While neither of us ever spoke about it, we were always on the lookout for the one track that only the two of us knew about—the track of an old cougar who had one leg shorter than the others.

Earlier in the summer, a cougar had begun to hunt sheep. There was a huge hunt, and the cougar had been killed, finally. We'd seen it ourselves.

Only it hadn't been the wily, legendary old cougar. It had been one of the cougar's offspring who had never really learned to hunt on its own. The old cougar had tried to protect it, but hadn't been able to in the end.

Now only Ashley and I knew the old cougar was still out there. And we always kept a lookout for its track. We'd never found it. But that didn't keep us from looking.

"I'm not sayin' I'm gonna go climb up there," I said as we walked along. "Just that I'd *like* to."

"Yeah, but I know you, Josh," she warned. "Once you get your mind set on something . . ."

"Not this time, don't worry. Ruth says you can't get to the eyrie. She says it's too hard a climb."

Ashley snorted. "But I'll just bet you're already trying to figure ways to get there, aren't you?" She stopped and looked back.

I looked away. She was right, of course. I *was* figuring ways to get there. I'd been looking through climbing books and books about eagles and other birds that Mark kept in the library.

It would be very, very hard. No question about it. But not impossible. People had climbed up to eagle eyries. It could be done.

"Oh, you know, it can't really be done," I muttered.

"But you're lookin', aren't you?" Ashley demanded.

I finally stared back. "Even if I am, so what? It's just for fun. I wouldn't actually try anything."

"You'd better not," Ashley said sternly. "Your mom would go absolutely, totally bonkers. You know she would."

"Yeah, I know," I sighed.

I let it drop after that. I really had no intention of trying anything. But it was fun to think about, nevertheless.

We caught a trail of mule deer finally. There were at least six of them, maybe seven, all does. Two of them were small. They'd probably been fawns in the spring and were only now learning how to live on their own.

Deer don't ever really live on their own, though. Not like other animals. They tend to stick together, like a herd of cattle or sheep will. They'll wander

21

through the forest in a group of up to ten or eleven, nibbling for food.

I'd put a salt lick out back of our house earlier in the summer. Around suppertime, I usually tossed out some corn in the back. The deer always came, like clockwork. They were no longer afraid.

I'd given each of them names. I practically knew each one of them, like you know your dog. I couldn't get close enough to pet them, but they didn't mind now when Mom or I went out on the back porch to watch.

A deer was a funny creature. It was as skittish as any animal I'd watched, even though it had almost nothing to be afraid of. I always got a kick out of watching how the mule deer in the Sierras bounded away on all fours, which was different from the way the white-tailed deer of the East sort of loped away.

There really wasn't much that hunted it down, not even out in the deep wilderness. The occasional cougar or bear went after them. But more deer were killed by cars, disease, or starvation in the winter than anything else.

The mule deer Ashley and I were tracking almost certainly were not the same group, though, that came out to my back yard every night. We were too far from Ganymede.

We followed the tracks for at least a mile, to an open meadow in the heart of the forest. They were just basically hanging out, like we were.

Ashley and I crept up on them. We were downwind, so they couldn't smell us. As long as we were quiet, we could get pretty close. We both tried not to step on any fallen branches, which would startle them.

We got right up to the edge of the meadow before

one of them sensed us. All of the deer jerked their heads up at the same moment, their ears high, on alert. Several of them started shifting their heads back and forth.

Silently, the word went out. Danger lurked nearby. First one of them started to meander away, then another. Within seconds, all of them had bounded away from the meadow. They were gone in a flash.

Who knew what had alerted them to our presence? I had no idea. We hadn't made a sound. Yet they'd known we were close by. Some sixth sense had told them. That's what amazed me about animals.

"Come on, let's head back," Ashley said.

I stood up. "Yeah, might as well, now that you've scared 'em off."

"No way," she protested. "They heard your wheezin'."

"You were the one huffin' and puffin'."

"Not me. I didn't make a sound."

A sudden sharp *crack* of a single-shot rifle broke through our argument. The sound came from a long way off. But I knew what the sound was from. The hunters were at it again.

"No!" I yelled out.

"They can't hear you." Ashley frowned. "They're too far."

"I don't care," I said angrily. I started to run in the direction of the sound. Ashley followed behind.

"Wait up," she called out. "Where are you goin', anyway?"

There was a second shot. There was the *crack*, followed by a metallic, ringing echo through the valley. There was no way to tell whether the hunter had hit anything.

23

I ran even faster. I had no idea where I was going, of course. I just wanted to do something, and this was all I could think of.

It took Ashley a little while to catch me. When she did, she started tugging on my shirt sleeve. "Stop," she said, out of breath. "Josh, stop for a sec."

I finally came to a reluctant halt. I was very much out of breath. I doubled over, grabbed the bottom of my shorts, and caught my breath. Ashley stood beside me, breathing hard.

"You're crazy, you know that?" Ashley said finally.

"I know."

"There's no way you can get to where the hunter's firing. No way, not in a million years."

"But I have to do something."

"Not from here you can't."

"But . . ."

"Look," Ashley said impatiently. "Go talk to Mr. Wilson about it. Maybe he can help. But running around out here is stupid. You can't do anything this way."

Ashley was right, of course. This *was* pretty silly. It was just that I hated the thought of someone taking an eagle out of the sky just for the sport of it. That just seemed wrong to me.

There was a third shot, followed quickly by a fourth. But I stayed put. The shots were several miles away, at least. It would take me hours to get anywhere near them.

And I had no idea what I'd actually do if I did get near them. It wasn't like I could stop the hunters or anything. I had no way to do that.

"All right. I'll go see Mr. Wilson. You wanna come with me when I do?"

"When?"

"This afternoon, after lunch?"

"OK. Can your mom drive us to the ranger station?"

"Sure." Mom always agreed to do stuff like that. Even when she didn't want to.

"Great," Ashley said. "We'll meet at your house."

$\triangle$

CHAPTER 6

$\triangle$ Mom was not thrilled, however. Not thrilled at all.

"Josh," she said with a pained sigh. "I can't just run you out to the ranger station every time you get the itch to ask Mr. Wilson something."

"But this is important."

"I'm sure it is," Mom said somewhat sarcastically.

"I wanna talk to him about the hunter."

"What hunter?"

"The one that's going after the eagles, near Cascade Mountain."

"What in the world are you talking about?"

I told her what we'd heard, and what Ruth and I had talked about. Mom listened patiently, like she always did. She never interrupted me, even when I was rambling.

"So you're sure about this?" she asked when I was finished.

"Yeah, I'm sure. So is Ruth. Ashley heard the shots, too."

Mom looked at me. "Could be a rancher, you know, firing at something on his property."

"I don't think so. The sound carried a long way. It was someone hunting up high. Had to be."

Mom was quiet for a few seconds. "Don't get carried away with this, Josh."

"Mom, I won't."

"You'll get going on this—"

"Don't worry. I won't."

Mom shook her head. She did know me. "There's nothing you can do about this. Just leave it to the rangers. This is something for Mark and Mr. Wilson to deal with."

"That's why I want to talk to them, to tell them about what I saw and heard," I said insistently.

Mom laughed. She could see I wasn't about to give up. "All right, let's go. I assume Ashley's coming with us, too?"

I nodded. "She'll be here in a sec."

"You were pretty sure about this, weren't you?"

I grinned. "Yep, I was."

Mom spent a lot of the trip there talking to me. She was tricky about it. She kept circling around, ducking in and out. But I got the basic point.

I had this *tendency* to kind of go off the deep end. I'd get really carried away with something, get really into it until there was no turning back. And she was afraid this was exactly the same kind of thing.

She was right. I could feel myself getting swept up in this. But I didn't know what to do about it. I hated the thought of some hunter just taking those eagles out for no good reason. I wanted someone to do something about it.

Mom kept coming back to how it was the job of the rangers to look out for things like that. But what if the rangers can't do that? I persisted. Then no one could, Mom said.

Mark was out repairing a trail with a whole bunch of the rangers when we arrived at Ranger Station #3. A storm had come through the past night, and lightning had taken out quite a few trees. Luckily, there had been no fires, which could have been real trouble.

This was the time of year when forest fires really got out of control, Mark said. The leaves hadn't fallen off the trees yet. They wouldn't for quite a few weeks. But the forest was very dry. A fire would spread quickly.

Mr. Wilson was in, though. He was in the main cabin at the station, looking over some reports of the storm damage.

Mr. Wilson was the grizzled veteran of the ranger corps. Once, when I'd first arrived, he and I had gone out together to look for a little boy who'd been mauled and dragged off by a crazed bear.

His Jeep had overturned, Mr. Wilson had been pinned beneath it, and I'd come face to face with the bear myself.

The incident had made us fast friends, even though we were years apart. There was a bond. We could both feel it, even though neither of us ever spoke about it. Mr. Wilson wasn't like that. Actually, I wasn't either.

He didn't even look up as we walked in. "Toss me that book," he barked at me.

"What book?" I asked.

"The brown one."

I scanned the closest desk. There was a smallish brown book in the center of it. I picked it up. "This one?"

"Is it brown?"

"Yeah."

"Do you see any other brown books around?"

I looked around the room. It was littered with maps and papers. But no brown books. "Nope. This is the only one."

"Then give it to me, already," he growled.

I smiled broadly. I glanced over at Ashley. She was smiling, too. I walked over to Mr. Wilson and handed the book to him. "Whatcha doin'?"

"Tryin' not to be bothered by pesky, bored, know-it-all kids," he answered.

"Like us, you mean?"

"Did I mention your name?"

Mom interrupted us. "Can I leave them with you?"

"Do you have to?" he grunted.

"Josh insisted," Mom laughed.

Mr. Wilson looked up. He looked first at my mom, then at Ashley, and finally at me. "This must be important if you made a trip all the way out here. You haven't been here in a little while. I wondered what happened to you."

I'd worked at the ranger station for a few weeks earlier this summer, until Mark said I should take a break to enjoy the summer before school started.

"Yeah, well, I had a few questions," I said.

Mr. Wilson glanced over at my mom. "They'll be fine. Mark can take 'em home."

Mom nodded. "No trouble, you hear me?"

"Got it." I nodded. "See ya."

"Thanks for the ride, Mrs. Rawlings," Ashley said.

"My pleasure, Ashley," Mom said. "So nice to see at least one of you has manners."

I ignored the barb and turned to Mr. Wilson. I waved to Mom as she left.

"So are you trackin' those hunters?" I asked Mr. Wilson.

"What hunters?"

"What hunters?" I almost exploded. "Are you kiddin'? You can practically hear 'em all over the place. I bet you can hear 'em all the way down the valley of the Kaweah River."

Mr. Wilson nodded. "Shoot, you're probably right. I'll bet you can hear 'em in Fresno, right?"

"Come on! I'm serious."

"I can see that."

"So have you heard 'em, or not?"

Mr. Wilson looked up very briefly. "Yes, Josh, we've all heard the rifle shots."

"So?"

"So what?"

"What are you doin' about it?" I practically yelled in his ear.

Mr. Wilson stopped looking at his reports on the storm damage. He pushed his glasses a little farther down on his nose and glared at me over the top of the rims. "And what, *exactly*, would you have us do about it?"

I stood my ground. I wanted answers. "I dunno. Something. Couldn't you, like, set up patrols who could keep track of the eagles and watch for the hunters?"

Ashley chimed in. "Yeah, they're around Cascade Mountain, aren't they? Couldn't you set up regular patrols around there?"

Mr. Wilson stared back at both of us like we'd completely lost our minds. "You're serious?"

"Yeah, we're serious," I said quickly. Ashley nodded in agreement.

Mr. Wilson put his books off to the side. "Josh, how far away is Cascade Mountain from here, do you figure?"

I shrugged. "Five miles?"

"As the crow flies, maybe"—he nodded—"or as the eagle flies, I guess. But we're not eagles. We're people —rangers—who have to drive four-wheel vehicles to certain parts of the forest."

"So you can—"

Mr. Wilson put his hand up, cutting me off. "But we can't drive any of those over to Cascade Mountain. It's too far into the range. It's just about the highest point on the Great Western Divide in this part of the Sierra Nevadas."

"But you can see Cascade Mountain from the valleys, practically."

"Come on, Josh!" He scowled. "You've been here long enough. You know better. Just because you can see that peak doesn't mean you can get there easily."

Mr. Wilson was right. You could see almost all of the high peaks along the Great Western Divide from a long way off—the ones that were 11,000 or 12,000 feet high, at least.

The Great Western Divide was a range of mountains that went right through the heart of the Sierra Nevadas beginning near the High Sierra National Park, which ran right through the Sequoia, Kings Canyon, and Yosemite national parks.

There were more than a dozen peaks visible from almost anywhere in the national parks, including Cascade Mountain. Only Mount Whitney, which was the tallest mountain in the continental United States, wasn't visible unless you went up and over the smaller mountains in the divide.

Which you had to do by foot. Mr. Wilson was right, of course, and I knew it. There wasn't a single road that went across the Sierra Nevada mountain range. Not a single one. If you wanted to go from Fresno east directly through the mountains, you had to hike. Or take a pack train. You couldn't drive.

Just a couple of paved roads actually went from the foothills, where Ashley and I lived, into the beginning of the mountain peaks. From there you had to walk to get up and over the Great Western Divide and into the deep mountains and then, eventually, to the other side and the desert.

Cascade Mountain was right smack-dab in the heart of the Great Western Divide. There was no easy way to get to it, other than to take a meandering six- or seven-mile path to it.

The path worked its way back and forth along several mountain slopes overlooking steep canyons. I guess I knew that. But I still wanted Mr. Wilson to *do* something.

"Awright, I know," I grumbled. "Just cause you can see it doesn't mean you can get there real easily."

"It's a day hike to get there, Josh, and you know it."

"Yeah, I know."

"So it isn't easy to keep track of what's going on near it, now, is it?"

"No, I guess not," I admitted.

"But there are rangers out there sometimes, aren't there?" Ashley interjected.

"Sure," Mr. Wilson agreed. "But so what? We're

33

only in that area on occasion, when we need to be. Not enough to keep track of hunters trying to take eagles down."

"But you could look, couldn't you?" Ashley persisted.

Mr. Wilson sighed. "Look, kids. I know you both have the best of intentions here. I want to see those eagles survive, too, just like you. But the fact of the matter is this. And it's simple. If someone wants to take a high-powered rifle to the slopes of Cascade Mountain—which is a good day hike from here—set up camp and start hunting them, there isn't much you or I can do about it."

"But Mr. Wilson, they've had babies," Ashley groaned.

"I know," Mr. Wilson said softly. "We've heard there may be two that made it this year."

"So you *have* to do something to protect them," Ashley persisted.

Mr. Wilson walked over to a big topographical map spread out across the far end of the main cabin. He waved at both of us. "Come here. I want you to see this clearly."

We both ambled over. "Yeah, I've seen this a hundred times," I grumbled.

"Well, let me show it to you for the hundred and first time," he said sharply. Mr. Wilson pointed to a red X on the map. "This is us. We're right here." He traced a dotted line along the map. "And here's an old logging trail that the rangers can take a four-wheel on."

The dotted line stopped well short of the high mountain ranges. I could see what Mr. Wilson was driving at. I guess he just wanted us to see it for our-selves.

"From the end of this logging trail—from the end of this dotted line—to Cascade Mountain is a series of switchbacks up and over a whole bunch of ranges," he continued. "Getting to Cascade Mountain is no easy task."

"OK, we can see that," I said irritably.

"I mean, it's a very *difficult* task," Mr. Wilson said, his eyes burning now. "It would take half of my rang-ers to patrol Cascade Mountain. They'd have to stay out there in the wilderness overnight to do it. They'd have to go out in shifts, stay out a few days at a time, and then return."

"So you could do it, if you had to?" I asked blankly.

Mr. Wilson jabbed an angry finger at the map. "Josh! Look again! Yes, of course, we could do it, if we had to. If there was an emergency of some sort. We could send the rangers into the range, have them set up a little camp. But I can't do that."

"Why not?" I asked.

"Because I have a responsibility to look after the entire park, not just one small portion of it. It's a huge park, as you well know, and I only have a handful of rangers to cover it."

"But this is important," Ashley persisted.

"We can't baby-sit one mountain in the middle of the wilderness," Mr. Wilson said with finality. "We can't, and both of you know it."

"Well, somebody has to do something to protect those eagles, if you won't."

"Josh, listen to me," Mr. Wilson said, closing his eyes. "I didn't say we wouldn't. I said it was very, very difficult. Not impossible. Just very hard."

"So you'll at least try?" I said hopefully.

Mr. Wilson sighed. I could be a real pain. "Yes, we'll try. If a ranger's going into the area anyway, I'll make sure he looks out for those eagles."

Ashley and I both grinned. That was at least something. I knew in my heart that it wasn't enough. But it was a start.

△

CHAPTER 7

△ First thing next morning, I went to visit Miss Lily. I didn't tell Ashley, Mom, or Mark. I didn't want anyone to know. I had a few questions, and I didn't want anyone hearing them.

They were innocent questions. But somebody might figure out what I had in mind. I didn't have it all sorted out just yet. But I was thinking—real hard.

Miss Lily was an ancient Indian. I think she was a Yokut. Once, there were lots of Yokuts in this part of California. But over the years, they'd all drifted away. There were no more Yokuts in the Sierra Nevadas.

Except Miss Lily, who lived in an old, weather-beaten hut on a piece of land that now belonged to the federal government. But the government looked the other way and didn't say anything to Miss Lily.

Actually, Mark said there were all sorts of weird places like that throughout the national parks. Some old-timers lived in cabins tucked away in the parks.

They all had 99-year leases that they'd gotten for almost nothing. When the leases expired, or when the old-timers in the cabins died, the government took them back.

Miss Lily didn't live on one of those 99-year leases. But she might as well have. The park rangers didn't mind her. She was harmless and, if anything, she was a huge help to them because she cared so much for her little plot of the earth.

Flowers grew like crazy in Miss Lily's part of the world. During the spring and summer, they were in bloom all over the place. Miss Lily tended to her little meadow like it was a garden, removing anything that might harm it.

If there was too much undergrowth in the forest nearby, Miss Lily would spend an afternoon or a week —whatever it took—to clear the underbrush and spread it around on the forest floor.

If a tree branch fell in a storm, she'd chop it up into little pieces and use it for firewood. If a storm flooded an area, she'd build trenches to run the water off to other parts of her little plot.

She was a true caretaker. I didn't know if Miss Lily had ever read the Bible. We'd never talked about God, really. But I could see that she had it just about right.

It was her duty to look after the earth. She didn't worship it. But she looked after it. She cared for it, the only way she knew how.

Over the course of the summer, I'd slowly come to the realization that there was something stirring inside me, something I'd never thought about before. I couldn't put it into words yet, exactly. But it was there nevertheless.

It had something to do with believing in God. I

looked at nature and I could see it. No, actually, I looked at the endless sea of pines on a mountain slope, or the raw, alpine peaks of the mountains, or the deep valley of the Kaweah River, or huge boulders that formed around the springs, and I *knew*.

I knew there was a Creator. This didn't all happen by accident. Nature wasn't some weird gyroscope thing that just sort of all jumbled together. Everything was too perfect. It all had purpose and meaning.

They say that some of the older redwoods in the sequoia groves have lived for more than two thousand years. That means that some of them were standing when Jesus Christ walked the earth.

That kind of blew my mind. When Jesus was telling people how they could be forgiven by God and live forever if they would give their lives over to Him, some of the same redwoods in the forests I walked through now were actually standing.

The wilderness can be a harsh place. But it is also a place where you retreat and go to when you need to really *understand* why we're here on the earth and what our place is.

It didn't surprise me that Jesus went into the wilderness for forty days before He started telling people about how they could have eternal life. It didn't surprise me at all. In fact, I would have been surprised if He *hadn't* spent time in the wilderness.

For it is out in the wilderness, where you have no shelter and no buffer between you and the elements, that you finally come to grips with the basic, mind-numbing fact: You are alone in the world. Just you, in the middle of the awesome creation. But the creation belongs to God, and you belong to God—so it is not something to be afraid of.

Just as there is beauty and purpose in the lilies of the field, there is beauty and purpose in what you do on the earth as well. You are part of the awesome creation.

As always, Miss Lily was toiling in her meadow when I arrived. She was bent over, working away at something.

"Whatcha doin'?" I asked quietly as I neared her.

Miss Lily looked up briefly. "Your eyes are covered by mist?"

"Well, um, no."

"So?"

I looked harder. There was a cloth of some sort to one side. Piled high on it were a bunch of leaves. As we spoke, she continued to gather up fallen leaves by hand and place them on the pile.

"You're gathering leaves," I declared.

"Yes, of course, but why?"

I glanced around the little meadow. In some parts, there were a lot of leaves. It was starting to become that time of year when all the leaves fell. Miss Lily was clearing her meadow as they fell.

"You wanted to get rid of some of the leaves?"

"Very good. Why?"

I thought for a moment. I knew that fallen leaves were a good compost and helped other things in the forest grow as a result. But if there were too many leaves? "To make sure you don't have too many leaves on the ground, which would choke things?"

Miss Lily smiled. "Very good. A little is a good thing. Too much is not."

I began to help her. She was gathering leaves that had drifted into high piles in some parts of the meadow and spreading them in the parts where there were no leaves. I moved to another section and began to carry armloads from one part of the meadow to another.

After a half an hour of this, she finally stood up. "Enough for now. Thank you, Joshua. You have been a help."

I followed her back to her ramshackle hut out in the middle of the meadow. It wasn't much to look at, but it was all Miss Lily had. She did the very best she could with it.

I worried about her with the winter coming on. But I knew she'd been here forever, and the winters weren't all that harsh here in the lower foothills. In the high, alpine reaches of the mountains, the winters were brutal. But they weren't so bad down here, where the snow rarely got very high.

"So why have you come, son of the earth?"

"Son of the earth?" I asked her.

Miss Lily settled into her rickety chair on her little front porch. The chair listed slightly to one side. I plopped down beside her. "How long have you been here?" she asked.

"In California?"

"Yes, here, in the mountains."

"Oh, I guess about four months."

"And when you came here, did you know much about the ways of animals or the forest?"

I laughed. "No, I was a total waste. I couldn't tell a pine tree from a redwood. Or a badger from a marmot."

"And now?"

"Now I know my way around."

She nodded. "You know the ways of animals."

"Some. There is still an awful lot more I want to learn."

"Yes, there is always more. You will never learn enough. But you have at least learned enough to walk the earth without disturbing it."

I thought about that for a second. "I see what you're saying. Some people, if they don't really know better, walk along in nature and sort of trample things as they go. Or they litter."

"Yes, or they just don't see what's there before their eyes."

"And I'm not like that?"

"Not anymore."

I liked that. I imagined that there were Indians, once, who were like that. Sons of the earth. They were not blind as they walked through nature.

"So why have you come to see me?" Miss Lily continued.

I hesitated only briefly. "What do you know about eagles?"

"Which kind?"

"Golden."

"Not the one that your country uses as its . . . its . . ."

"Symbol?" I said, finishing her sentence. I noticed, in passing, that she called it my country, not hers. "No, not the bald eagle. I'm interested in the golden eagle, the one that hunts in the mountains and the wilderness."

"Why are you curious?"

I looked away. I wasn't prepared to answer that, exactly. "Oh, just because. There are some hunters, I think, who are trying to kill a couple."

Miss Lily nodded. "I see. And you want to help?"

"Something like that."

She leaned back in her chair and thought for a moment. "Eagles are not what people think they are."

"And what is that?"

"They aren't the big hunters that some think."

"You mean they don't hunt down sheep? Stuff like that?"

"Yes, like that. Once, your people killed very many of them."

"Because they thought they were like mountain lions, who went after sheep and cattle?"

"Yes, like that."

"But they don't do that, is that what you're saying?"

"Yes, that is it. The eagle will take down a deer that is falling—"

"Falling?"

"One that is sick."

"Oh, yeah, I see."

"An eagle usually hunts the snake. Or the turtle."

"It can see those from the sky?"

"Eagles have great sight."

"Is that how it hunts? From the sky?"

Miss Lily nodded solemnly. "Yes, from very high up. It soars with its wings out, its beak down. It looks for movement on the ground. When it sees it, then it will strike."

"But not the bigger animals?"

"Not the bigger animals. That is right."

I began to zero in on what I was really curious about. "What about the babies?"

"A baby eagle?"

"Yeah, you know, like after they're a few months old, what are they like? Can they live on their own?"

"Have you watched birds as they nest?"

I shook my head. "A little. Not much."

"In the summer, birds build their nests. They lay their eggs. The little ones are born. They learn to live on their own in the summer."

"Yeah, I've seen some of that."

"But eagles are different."

"Different?"

"Because they must learn to hunt on their own. They learn from their parents. They must learn how to hunt from the sky. It is not an easy thing. Even for an eagle."

"Hm," I grunted. "So a baby eagle needs its parents."

"For a time."

"How long a time?"

"I do not know. Until it is ready to fly—and kill—on its own."

"Would you think that a baby eagle could make it right now?"

"Without its parents?"

"Yeah, if a baby eagle had been born this spring, and its parents were killed, could it survive?"

Miss Lily looked at me more closely. "Because?"

"Just because."

"I have not seen an eagle around here for a very long time. But your eyes tell me that there is a new eagle in the world. Yes?"

I looked her in the eye. "Yes, there is a new eagle in the land. Maybe two."

Miss Lily's eyes grew wide. "Two. That does not happen much."

"I know. That's what the rangers say."

"And there are two?"

"I don't know for sure. But that's what people say."

"And they are where?"

I gestured over my shoulder, toward the east. "Up on Cascade Mountain."

"Cascade Mountain? I do not know the names you have given to the mountains around here."

I thought for a moment. "It's the mountain that has this really huge waterfall coming down one side of the mountain, across some black rocks on the western side."

"Yes, I know it. The Mountain of Falling Waters."

I smiled. Miss Lily always saw things from a different perspective. "Yes, Falling Waters. That's the one."

"And there are eagles near it?"

"Yes, I think so. Up at the top."

"And the parents are in danger?"

"Um, yeah, I think so. We've heard hunters with rifles."

"Yes, the long-fire."

"Long-fire?"

"The fire that comes from a long way off. Guns, you call them."

"Yes, guns. They have guns. That's what they're trying to kill the eagles with."

"Joshua, you cannot stop those with guns. If they mean to kill, they will kill."

I looked down at the rough floor of her porch. "I know. I wish I could do something, but I can't."

"But you are concerned about the babies, is that it?"

"Yeah, something like that."

Miss Lily remained quiet for a long time. I didn't disturb her. "I think," she said finally, "that a baby

45

eagle will wait for a very long time. A very long time. Too long, maybe."

"Wait? For its parents?"

"Yes, when they are not hunting with their parents, they will wait in the nest. And then, when winter comes, they will not know how to hunt when the ground is covered with snow."

I thought I understood. "So if the parents were killed, you'd have to get the babies to leave the nest? And then they'd have to learn how to hunt with snow on the ground?"

"Either that, or they'd have to hunt in a place where the ground was not always covered with the white snow."

"Like near here? Near where we live?"

"Yes, like that. But Joshua, that is not an eagle's home. An eagle lives in the mountains, with the rocks. Not here."

"I know that," I said solemnly.

Miss Lily stood up to go gather more leaves. "You must not try to reach those eagles. It is not possible. Let nature take care of its own, in the way of the earth."

"I, um, I don't know that I can do that," I said fiercely. "I have to do something."

"They are very high up. Not where a person can go."

"I can climb."

"Not to where the eagles live, you cannot."

"Yes, you can now. There's equipment that lets you climb across rocks."

Miss Lily put an old, feeble hand on my shoulder. I didn't flinch or try to pull away. "You should not do this. Or even think about it. The eagles must live on their own. You cannot change their fate. That is the way of the earth."

I gritted my teeth. I knew she was right. But I *had* to do something. What I hadn't figured out was *what,* exactly.

△
CHAPTER 8

△ Ruth had told me a hundred times. No, maybe a thousand times. *Never* climb alone. It was the way climbers got killed.

There was this guy in California who called himself the Daredevil. The newspapers had written all sorts of stories about him because he could climb these steep mountain faces by himself, without ropes or pitons or anything to support him.

They found him dead at the bottom of about a 4,000-foot mountain one day. He'd slipped and fallen. That was that.

So don't ever climb alone, Ruth warned me. Over and over. I knew it. I understood it.

But there was a way to climb solo that was fairly safe. Ruth even did it sometimes, if she was going up a rock face and then coming back down it, and she wasn't too high up.

"Why do *you* climb by yourself sometimes, if you

won't let me do it?" I asked her eight days before our climb on Cascade Mountain.

"I'm an expert, that's why," she growled at me.

"But I'm pretty good."

"Pretty good isn't good enough. Not for a solo. You need to have it all together. You need everything to be exactly right. Because if it isn't, you're dead."

Actually, rock climbing—the kind I did—wasn't really all that dangerous. It just looked like it. Mark and Mom wouldn't let me go if it wasn't safe.

When you climbed in a group like I did, with an expert lead climber like Ruth, there was really no way you were going to get in trouble. I was always hooked to so many safety ropes, the entire mountain would have to fall over before I was going to get hurt. There was just no way all of those ropes would come loose at once and let me fall.

Climbing solo was something else entirely, though.

The really crazy solo climbers did something called "aided climbing." Why they called it "aided" was beyond me, because the way they went about getting from one place to another on the rock face wasn't aided by much.

They would climb up as high as they could, hammer in their piton, click their rope in place, and loop their rope through. Then they'd use their hammer to reach up higher, step on the piton, and climb up.

They'd look for the next spot to put a piton in place. But the only thing that kept them from falling was the piton they were standing on. That was it. Just the one piton. If it broke free, they fell. No ropes or safety loops. That was it.

That kind of solo climbing was clearly crazy. Ruth said the only climbers she knew who did that were young and stupid. They thought they would live forever. They didn't think beyond the next handhold on the rock face.

The other way to climb by yourself that wasn't as crazy—the kind Ruth did—was to start at the bottom of a cliff face and climb up using pitons and rope, but leaving them all in place so that if one broke free, then all of the others held you in place.

If you used a sturdy rope, and you kept all the pitons in place, then you had plenty of protection. The only problem with that, of course, was that you had to reverse your climb on the way back *down*. And that was hard, Ruth said. Much harder than going up.

Plus, if the climb was high at all, you might end up stuck on the rock face when it got dark. Now, that was interesting. What were you supposed to do if it got dark and you were stranded up there? I asked her.

"You're not there in the first place," Ruth said, glaring at me from a spot about five feet above me on Splinter Rock, a neat little mountain face that was just high enough to be fun. It was about a two-mile hike from the end of one of the paved roads that went into the national park, so the only people who came by were occasional day hikers.

"Yeah, but what if you were?" I called up.

"*You* wouldn't be."

"I know, I know. But what if you were there, what would you do?"

Ruth clicked and snapped to make sure she was secure, and then dropped down next to me. She did everything so quickly, fluidly, that it always took my breath away. One minute she was standing five feet above me, the next she was hanging right beside me. Sort of like a spider.

51

"Look, you!" she said, looking me directly in the eye. "You're just a twelve-year-old kid. You're gonna be a pretty good rock climber someday. But not if you start thinking about fool things like this."

I tried hard not to look away. Ruth wasn't much bigger than me, but she had muscles bulging everywhere. Her arms were probably twice as big as mine. Her legs were like pile drivers. She could probably stomp me if she absolutely had to.

"I'm not—"

"I don't care," she said, cutting me off. "All I'm saying is this: Don't even think about it. If I thought you were going to try something, I'd stop the lessons right now."

"I'm not," I said quickly. "Don't worry. I'm just curious."

Ruth stared at me. She was trying to read me. She was pretty good at it. I didn't mind, because I wasn't exactly sure what I had in mind. I *was* only curious. I didn't have a plan.

But there was something. It was only in the back of my mind. I didn't really let myself think about it too much. Yet it was there. A little.

Ruth swung over about as close as you could get. She reached out and gripped my shirt and tugged on it. "Climbing like that is dangerous, kid. Real dangerous. Don't even dream about it."

"But *you* do it," I persisted.

"Like I said. I'm a pro. I know what I'm doing. I've been at this for a long, long time. I know how to do it safely, by the book."

"And I couldn't learn?"

Ruth gripped my shirt harder. "You will. But only with practice. A *lot* of practice, with me and your stepdad and some of the rangers and other climbers by your side. Not by yourself."

"OK, already." I swallowed hard. "I was only curious."

"Curious, huh?" Ruth grunted. "I know you, Josh. You're cooking something up. You always do."

"I'm not!" I protested.

"Yeah, well, don't," Ruth said, pushing away. With three quick pulls on the rope, she was back up to her previous position and continued the climb.

△

CHAPTER 9

△ On Saturday, seven days before our climb and just ten days before the start of school, Ashley and I spotted one of the baby eagles. I was certain of it.

We were out on a long day hike, at least four miles into the national park. We were on a well-marked trail that led up into a white rock canyon. There had been an old cabin and a mine in the rocks, once. The miners had never found anything, and the mine was all sealed up now, but it was still a cool place to explore.

You could see Cascade Mountain from the canyon. Actually, you could see almost every single one of the big mountain peaks on the Great Western Divide, once you got high enough in the canyon to peer out over the edge toward the divide.

I'd never been over on the other side, to the east of the Sierra Nevadas. Because there were no roads that went from the western side of the Sierra Nevada in the national parks to the eastern side, near Mount Whitney and into the desert, I'd never been there.

One day, Mark told me, we'd hike the entire length of the High Sierra trail, from the trailhead to Mount Whitney. It was just over seventy miles, and it took about a week. Maybe next summer, he told me.

I didn't know what the divide looked like from the east, but from the west, you could see at least twelve of the peaks—like Cascade Mountain—that went up close to 12,000 feet.

I was sitting on a big rock in the middle of a cool stream, drinking water from a tin cup I always packed with, when I spotted the eagles. They were way, way up, the baby eagle and one of its parents.

From where we were sitting, you could just barely tell that one of them was smaller. They flew quite close together. The baby flew above and slightly off to one side of its parent.

"Look!" I said, pointing to the sky. Ashley looked up sharply from another rock in the middle of the stream.

"What?" She stared hard, and then spotted them as well. "Oh, cool. That's neat."

"Those are eagles, right?"

"Yeah, they have to be." She nodded. "Look how big they are."

"You don't think they're vultures, do you?"

"Nah. Look how high up they are. Vultures don't go that high."

Ashley was right. They were *way* up there. It had to be the eagle, with its baby.

Just then, a second bird came hurtling from another direction. It was moving like crazy. It raced toward the first two birds. I'd never seen anything move so fast.

An instant later, a fourth bird came trailing behind. It was clearly trying to keep up with the third one, but it was lagging behind quite badly.

"What's goin' on?" Ashley called out to me. "Do you see that?"

"Yeah, I do," I said, straining hard to see.

"Are they attacking?"

"I don't know."

We both watched and held our breaths. The third bird came rushing toward the two eagles. It got closer and closer, and then swept right by. The eagles picked up their speed and followed.

The fourth bird, meanwhile, struggled to keep pace with the first three. That's when I figured it all out.

"There are two of them," I said to Ashley.

"Yeah, I can see that," she called back.

The rangers were right. Not one, but two baby eagles had been born that summer on Cascade Mountain. They were up there right now, flying with their parents. That's what we were watching.

It was rare these days that one baby golden eagle was born. But two? The old-timers said it had been years and years since that had happened. Some of them couldn't remember a time when it had happened, in fact.

Ashley and I watched the eagles drift back and forth across the clear blue cloudless sky for almost an hour. The eagles were clearly out for a stroll. They weren't hunting. They'd do that later, when it was dusk and some of the rabbits and rodents came out. Now, they were just hanging out. A mile up in the sky.

I wondered if the hunters I'd heard before were out here somewhere, with their sights on the eagles. Could bullets reach them? They were awfully high up.

I kind of doubted that anything could reach them from this distance, but I didn't really know.

Finally, the eagles returned to their mountain home. I watched them circle for a long time around a shrubless, treeless alpine peak with patches of white snow. I now had a pretty good idea where their eyrie was.

They'd chosen the highest, most remote part of Cascade Mountain for their eyrie. There was one part of the peak that jutted out from the rest. It was a jagged outcropping that you could see almost from the valley, it was so distinct.

The eyrie was somewhere near or on that outcropping, at the highest point of the mountain. I figured it was nearly impossible to reach without a long, long climb. No human had probably ever come near their eyrie.

Which was why they were there, of course. The eagles wanted solitude. They didn't want to be disturbed. They just wanted to hunt for rabbits at dusk, and to bomb across the sky during the day. Nothing more. Life was that simple.

A family of mule deer wandered by a short time later, after the eagles had landed. There were two bucks, four does, and three fawns, now almost grown. The bucks stayed off by themselves, nibbling at leaves. The does and fawns bounded along together.

Out here in the canyon, where very few people came by, the deer weren't at all skittish or afraid. They were more curious than anything. They'd probably seen day hikers before, out here every so often. They weren't threatened by us at all.

The deer went from bush to bush, nibbling away.

They glanced over their shoulders at us occasionally. Just to make sure.

A marmot popped up downstream. It had a mouthful of grass. It poked its head over the rock, stared at us a moment, ducked back in, then climbed all the way out and stood its ground on top of the rock.

The marmot let loose with a shrill whistle, and then ducked back inside its little rock home beside the stream.

Marmots were funny little creatures. They were part of the woodchuck family. Actually, the woodchuck was part of the *Marmota* family, but most people have never heard of marmots. They weren't afraid of people or camps at all. They loved to hang around.

A black-tailed jackrabbit made a sudden dash across the open canyon floor. Jackrabbits can hit a top speed of about thirty-five miles an hour when they're really moving.

This one was only cruising. It knew there were no predators out hunting just yet—how it knew that I couldn't say—so it was obviously in no hurry. But it still moved lickety-split, and vanished into a clump of bushes an instant later.

There was a short, piercing bleat about fifty feet away. Ashley and I glanced over at a rocky ledge. Sure enough, there were two pikas out on top, near a pile of grass. Pikas are about the size of chipmunks, but they look more like mice. Their bleat, though, is unmistakable. They really lay into you if you get too close.

Like the marmots, pikas prepare for the winter by "harvesting" fresh grass. They pile it up on the rocks during the day and "cure" it just the way farmers do. Then they store their "hay" in their dens among the rocks for the long, winter months.

At least four different kinds of birds flew past us while we were by the stream.

I could have stayed there forever, just watching each of the animals. Ashley could have, too. We didn't need to talk about it. We just knew it.

There wasn't any real story here. It wasn't like a TV show, where you had cars screeching around corners or people shooting at each other or anything like that. There was no beginning to a story like the one out here.

But there was no end, either. I knew that tomorrow, if I came out to this very same spot, I would likely see the deer family come meandering by again. The pikas would bleat at me again. I might see the jackrabbit, or I might not.

But they'd all be here, somewhere. This was their life, such as it was. It just happened. Every day. Much like today.

"Let's go," I called out to Ashley. "The sun's going down."

I took one last look toward Cascade Mountain and the eagles' home before we headed back. But they were safely in their eyrie now, and they wouldn't appear again until about dusk.

CHAPTER 10

△ I started preparing for our climb up Cascade Mountain on Monday, five days before we were actually supposed to go there.

Actually, what I did was pack and unpack about a thousand times. I kept seeing how much I could fit into my pack without it showing.

I packed an extra pair of wool socks, just in case it got extra cold at night. I wanted to be ready if we were somehow stuck out in the open, on a rock face, in the middle of the night.

I packed an extra pair of thermal underwear. It seemed like a luxury, but I hated the thought of getting cold. So I figured it was worth it to lug them along. I packed some gloves as well.

The hard part was the extra pitons and climbing gear. Ruth and my stepfather were planning to carry most of the heavy equipment. But I was bringing other junk along, like pitons and clips for the extra rope I was stowing. I had my own hammer.

I also brought a sling. Ruth said that climbers who went up sheer rock faces that took more than a day sometimes slept in a sling out on the face itself, hanging from the pitons. I couldn't even begin to imagine what that was like.

Food was hard to plan for. I thought and thought about what I could possibly bring with me.

Once you got to the alpine region of a mountain, everything stopped growing. The big pine trees and redwoods stopped at about 6,000 feet. The smaller pines and shrubs dropped off by 10,000 feet. Above that, there was nothing. Just snow and rock.

If I had to spend any time at all up there, I'd need to take food with me. I could always melt snow for my water. It would be gritty with dirt, but at least it would be water. Food, though, was a problem.

I finally decided to take a healthy supply of jerky with me, and some dried fruit. If I ran out, then I'd have to figure out how to find stuff from the forest; I'd done that before.

I didn't tell Ashley what I had in mind. She was mad enough already that she wasn't going on this climb. Oh, she understood that this was something I was doing with my stepdad. But that didn't mean she was happy about it.

Mr. and Mrs. Deaton were taking her up to Yosemite for a camping trip near the valley and the falls the last week of summer. But she was still unhappy. She wanted to go climbing with me. She'd already been to Yosemite.

I also packed a small pair of binoculars, which Mark had given me for Christmas. I hadn't used them much, but I figured they'd come in handy now. You could see for quite a ways with them.

I studied every book and topo map Mark had for Cascade Mountain. I wanted to know every inch of that mountain before we got there.

We were going around behind the mountain to climb up from the eastern side. It was an easier ascent, Ruth said. You could walk up to 10,000 feet without any trouble, really. We'd climb another thousand feet with ropes.

We weren't actually going anywhere near the peak of Cascade Mountain. That was too hard to get to, Ruth said. Plus, you could only get to it from the west, which was a very hard climb.

To get to the peak, you had to go up and over a ridge at the top, down into a valley between ridges that were covered with a sea of pines, up a second ridge, and then to a sheer rock face that went straight up to the peak. There was no path.

The peak itself was sheltered from the wind, except near the very top, because there were so many ridges that fronted it from several different directions.

You could only see the very top of the mountain from the valleys. Every other part of the mountain could be seen only from close up. It was a mountain within mountains, one of the more unusual peaks in the western divide.

Ruth said it would take us a full day to hike to 10,000 feet. We were going to set up camp and then climb the next day, if all went well. We'd go up, take a look around, climb back down, camp for a second night, and then return home on the third. School would start the next day.

I was having trouble thinking about school. So

much had happened to me during the summer. I had almost become a different person. I could recognize almost any animal track immediately. I knew what they were doing, when they were doing it.

I felt comfortable outside, even in the deep wilderness. It didn't scare me. I respected it. I knew there were grizzlies and cougars there, but I also knew that they would keep their distance from me. To them, I was a predator as well, to be avoided if at all possible.

I felt like I could survive in the wilderness on my own. I was certain of it. It wasn't something I wanted to do. But I knew I could do it. If I had to.

I finally left my pack alone. I'd put enough in it. I was prepared for almost anything—no matter what it was.

△

CHAPTER 11

△ "You ready?"

Mark shook me again, harder this time. I mumbled and tried to roll over. I'd been up half the night, tossing and turning. I just wanted to sleep some more.

"Hey! Let's go!" Mark said. "Ruth's waiting."

I bolted up and rubbed my eyes. I looked over at my stepdad. He was fully dressed and ready to go. I glanced out the window of my loft. It was still dark outside.

"Ummm," I mumbled. My mouth was dry. My tongue stuck to the roof of my mouth. "Is it time to go?"

"Yeah, sleepy," Mark laughed. "We gotta roll."

I tilted my head back and yawned wide. I stretched. Mark stood up and began to walk away. When I tried to put my head back on my pillow, he grabbed the covers and yanked them from the bed.

"Hey!" I complained. "It's cold!"

"I know. You'll be warmer once you're in your clothes. So move."

I rolled out of bed, shivering, and climbed into the double-stitch cotton shorts I was hiking in. I was going to wear a nice Gore-Tex shell while it was still dark and cold, and then stuff it into my pack when the sun was up.

I got into my clothes as fast as I could. Mark stood in the doorway long enough to make sure I was truly getting dressed.

"Breakfast's on the table," he called out as he descended the steps from my loft bedroom.

Mom was up, as usual, to see us off. Sometimes I kind of wished she'd go along on these trips with us. But Mom always said she was happy just to know that I was having fun. She claimed she didn't actually want to go herself.

I had a funny feeling that Mom could do just about anything she wanted, if she set her mind to it. When we went skiing, she was a whiz at it. She could go faster than me, when she tried.

After my dad died, Mom would even play catch with me sometimes. She wasn't exactly Ryne Sanberg, but she wasn't bad. She could catch even my hardest stuff, and she could throw it to me with something on it.

Mark told me that, before I was born, she'd trained for a marathon. She'd run for months just to get in shape for it. She'd finally run one, had done it under four hours, and then promptly retired from running.

I wondered sometimes why I didn't see more of that in her. Maybe it was because she spent all her time looking out for me. I don't know. I had trouble seeing her as anything other than my mom.

"Eat," she demanded of me. "You'll need your strength." Mom was sitting there, huddled in a big terry-cloth bathrobe. I knew she'd go climb back in bed after we left.

"I will," I muttered. I wasn't real hungry, but I knew I had to eat as much as I could now, before we started. I downed a big glass of orange juice first.

"You make sure you drink enough water, you hear me?" Mom said. "You'll cramp up, or get too tired otherwise. Even if it's cool out. All right?"

"Yeah, all right, already," I said irritably.

"I mean it," she said.

"I know." I crammed a muffin in my mouth. Mom watched me eat it. To make sure I ate enough before we left, I figured.

I walked over to the refrigerator to get another glass of orange juice. I opened the freezer and grabbed an ice cube. I waited until Mom had looked away from me, toward Mark, before I made my move.

It took me just three steps to get across the kitchen. I skidded to a stop behind Mom's chair and then deftly dropped the ice cube down her back.

She let out a long, terrible screech. She stood straight up, shaking like a tree in a storm. She yelled again, at the top of her lungs. The ice cube clattered to the floor an instant later.

She got to me before I could get clear of the kitchen and grabbed me from behind. "That was a cruel thing to do to your dear old mom so early in the morning," she said fiercely. She turned me loose an instant later, though.

"The two of you finished?" Mark asked. We looked at each other, and nodded. Then Mark quickly dropped his own ice cubes down our backs.

67

I got to Mark first and held him, while Mom gave him a good thumping on the back. It was a completely ridiculous way to start the morning. I was exhausted, and we hadn't even started. Oh well.

"Be careful," Mom said a few minutes later, after the car was packed and we were ready to leave. "Make sure you listen to Mark and Ruth. They know what they're doing."

"I will," I said.

"I mean it, Josh," she warned. "You listen to them."

"I will, Mom, don't worry."

"I always worry about you, Josh," she said somberly. "That's my job."

"Well, don't. I'll be all right."

Mark started the car. I hopped in quickly, waved at Mom, and we were off. She kept waving until we were out of sight.

CHAPTER 12

△ Ruth was waiting for us at the General Store, in the town of Jupiter. It was the easiest place to meet. She was sitting on the porch, sipping a cup of steaming coffee.

We still had a half-hour drive in front of us, at least. We had to go about five or six miles to the end of a twisting road that would take us as far as any paved road could go into the Sierra Nevadas. From there, we would trek to Cascade Mountain.

"Come on, we're losin' the sun already," Ruth said impatiently as she slid into the back seat.

I glanced around. It was still dark outside, though it was starting to get light in the east. "There's no sun yet," I laughed.

"There will be." Ruth frowned. "Soon. And we have a ways to go yet."

"Don't worry," I predicted confidently. "We'll make it, with plenty to spare."

Ruth cocked one eyebrow. "Oh? You've done this before?"

"I just know."

Mark didn't say anything. He just kept his eyes on the road. The road out of the foothills to the base of the Great Western Divide was a real monster, with several hundred hairpin turns. It took all his concentration to make sure we didn't drop over the edge of a cliff.

Ruth looked over at the backpack next to her in the back seat.

"Mark's?" she asked me.

"Yep. Mine's in the trunk."

"Did you pack right?"

"Just like you said." What I didn't tell her about was some of the extra equipment I was carrying, just to be on the safe side.

"Got your own piton bag? Rope belt? Extra pair of socks? Blister bandages?"

I nodded vigorously. "Yeah, I have everything. Don't worry. I made a list. I didn't leave anything off. I'm positive."

Ruth settled back into her seat. But she didn't sit there long. Ruth must have fidgeted a lot as a kid. She couldn't sit still to save her life.

Which was funny, really, because on the rocks she had the patience of Job. She could hang on a rock for ten minutes, waiting for someone below her to get settled or move up. It was here, though, where she wasn't actually doing anything, that she started to go stir-crazy.

I liked Ruth a lot. She was way too old to be a friend, but she was cool. She had it together. She knew what she was doing, and she did what she really wanted to.

I wanted to be like that when I grew up. I didn't want some stupid job that I hated, just because I had to make money. I wanted something that was fun, that was exciting. I wanted to wake up every morning the way I did now—wondering what was around the corner.

When I was in Washington, D.C., some of my friends had fathers who were never home. They worked all the time, like every night until it was really dark outside. And even when these dads were home, they were so tired they couldn't do anything for fun. They worked on Saturdays, and sometimes Sundays.

I thought that was dumb. Why would you do that? I stole a quick glance at Mark. I was glad he had the kind of job he did. He was around, even when he was working; I could go find him if I had to. I liked that.

"Whatcha thinkin' about?" Mark asked, his eyes still on the road.

"Oh, nothin'," I mumbled, suddenly embarrassed. I was glad people couldn't read minds.

"By the way," Mark continued, "some of the rangers told me they think we might run across a couple of interesting things up in the alpine meadows on Cascade."

"Yeah? Like what?" I said.

"Bighorn sheep, almost definitely. And elk, too."

"No way!" I said, suddenly excited. I'd studied the tracks for both, but I'd never actually seen either. You had to go up well into the mountains—to rocky ledges or mountain meadows—to catch sight of bighorn sheep. And elk were almost unheard of in this part of

California. There were only a few herds in California. Most of them were up in places like Oregon or Canada.

"And the rangers say the elk have brought other animals with them, like maybe wolverines," Mark added.

"Really?"

"Yeah, really." Mark smiled. "I think this could be quite a trip."

Wolverines, like the elk, were also quite rare in California. You almost never saw them here. They were mostly up in Canada. But it wasn't impossible.

Once, wolverines and elk and grizzly bears and all sorts of creatures roamed all over the West. But no more. Now, they were mostly just ghosts of the past, or pictures on pages. You had to go to zoos to see them.

The wolverine is unlike any other animal alive. It's three feet long, stocky, with short legs, small ears, and a short, bushy tail. But it is supposed to be the most ferocious animal in all of North America. It has bone-crushing teeth. It can bring an elk down, or drive a cougar away from a kill. Its hunting range is huge, like a thousand square miles. It just kind of lopes along until it finds something to kill and eat.

I hoped we wouldn't meet one. But I also secretly hoped that maybe we would. Mark had brought a gun along, just in case we came across something we couldn't handle. I'd fired a gun once in my life, and it had been out of sheer panic as a bear was charging me. I didn't ever want to do that again, as long as I lived. But I was glad Mark had one out here.

Only the rangers were allowed to carry weapons in the park wilderness. And even then, they could only carry them with special permission. Wild animals rarely, if ever, charged humans. You were better off clapping your hands or yelling at a bear than doing anything else. Wolverines, though, might be a different matter.

Interestingly, the wolverine's track looks a lot like a black bear's, only about half the size. They both have five toes with sharp claws, and a half pad that sinks into the ground when it lopes along. You could almost mistake a wolverine's track for a baby bear's if you weren't careful.

"Say, is Ashley OK about this?" Mark asked suddenly.

"She's all right, I guess. She really wanted to come along. But her folks are taking her to Yosemite."

"Oh, good. She'll like that."

"No, she won't!" I laughed. "She'd rather be here. She's seen Yosemite before."

Mark smiled. He knew Ashley like I did. Given a choice between something like Disneyland or climbing up some rocks in a gorge, she'd pick the gorge. Every time. "You can tell her all about it when you get back."

"Like she'll listen," I snorted.

"Hey, look!" Ruth said, pointing off to the side of the road. Mark eased the car into the next turnout on the road and pulled to a stop. We all looked out the window, over the sea of pines that covered the mountain slopes.

"What?" I asked.

"Across the way," Ruth said. "Do you see them bounding through the trees?"

We all looked harder. Then I saw them. You had to look closely to see them—it looked like a group of maybe twenty mule deer, traveling together. And they were really moving, bouncing at a fast clip through the trees.

"Must be running from something," Mark muttered.

"Yeah, they're goin' fast," Ruth said. "They're scared. That's a dead run for them, it looks like."

We watched the deer for a few minutes longer, until they were out of sight, and then continued the drive. As we got up close to 6,000 feet, I rolled the window down and hung my head out.

I loved the smell of the pines and redwoods up this high. It was a sweet smell, but not overpowering. It reminded me a little of the smell that I remembered coming from the kitchen when my dad was making waffles.

I closed my eyes. My dad. No matter how hard I tried to forget him, I couldn't. No matter how nice Mark was, I couldn't seem to wipe my dad from memory.

Mom said I shouldn't try. She said I should remember every single thing about him. They were all good memories, she said.

Maybe. I didn't know. It still hurt a little to remember him. Especially on trips like this, because those were the very best times we ever had together.

When Dad and I were out camping together, I always thought that it was exactly the way the world was supposed to be. Every moment, every step, every smell, every single word seemed just exactly right.

I didn't know, then, that was all I would have— those memories of what we were doing together. I thought that we'd do those things forever, that it would never end.

Mark slowed the car again. I pulled my head back inside. "What's up?"

"I wanted to show both of you something," Mark said mysteriously. "A couple of the rangers told me about it."

"What is it?" Ruth asked.

"You'll see." Mark pulled the car to a stop again. He climbed out. There was a natural spring nearby. We followed along behind as he clambered up and over some of the rocks to get near where the water tumbled out of the ground and down the mountainside.

There was a patch of long-stemmed, pale blue flowers. The leaves looked tough. They were shaped like swords.

"So?" I said.

"You don't know what these are?" Mark asked. He squatted to take a closer look at the flowers.

"Flowers," I said with a straight face. I wasn't, like, a huge fan of flowers. Animals were one thing. Flowers were something else entirely.

Miss Lily said I was looking at it exactly wrong. She said I had to learn *everything* about nature—the flowers included—before I could ever hope to get a really true picture of how it all worked together. But I ignored her. Flowers were still flowers as far as I was concerned.

"It's a Rocky Mountain iris, isn't it?" Ruth said, standing at my side.

I looked up at her and frowned. "How do you know about things like that?"

"I pay attention," Ruth answered.

Mark beamed. "Yes, exactly. It's a Rocky Mountain iris."

75

"But I thought they didn't grow around here," Ruth said.

"They don't," Mark offered. "Only in this one place, for some reason. A ranger spotted them here, and passed the word. Somebody probably carried the corms to here, for whatever reason."

"Isn't it late for these flowers to bloom like this?" Ruth asked.

Mark nodded again. "Yep. Sure is. They should have bloomed in May or July, maybe early August. But here it is the end of summer, and they're blooming. Go figure."

I stared at the pale blue flowers. I still couldn't see the big deal. It looked a whole lot like any old blue flower. Oh well.

There were no more big surprises on the way. I thought I saw a bobcat, briefly, through the trees. It jumped from a small ledge beside the road. It wasn't much bigger than a house cat, but it was twice as fast.

We parked beside a pack station at the end of the road. There were several trailheads that led off into the wilderness from there. I'd hiked several of them already since coming to California, including one that had led through a snow-filled pass.

"Hey, I never asked before—how come we aren't packing to Cascade Mountain?" I looked longingly at some of the mules and horses grazing peacefully in a steep, fenced pasture close by. It would be nice to ride to Cascade.

"I never pack, unless I have to," Ruth said. There was an edge to her voice I hadn't heard before.

"Why?"

"God gave us two legs. We can use them," she answered.

"But—"

"We're walking. That's it. Only the tourists use those beasts," she said.

I looked over at my stepdad for help. He shrugged and started to unpack the car. The first thing he did, though, took me by surprise. He unraveled some chicken wire. It was about three feet high, and he'd rolled enough to wrap around the car.

"What's that for?" I asked.

"Marmots," he said. He started at one end and rolled it around the entire car, so that it was touching the ground and extended up over the bottoms of the doors and the bumpers.

"What do ya mean, marmots?"

"They eat radiator hoses inside the engine."

"Oh, come on! You've gotta be kidding?"

"Nope. They like the salt or something."

"Really?"

"If you leave a car sitting like this, they'll come after it. The car won't start. They'll chew on everything they can get to."

"Man, that's crazy."

"It's what happens when animals spend too much time around us," Mark said as he tied the two ends of the chicken wire together with a small rope.

My pack felt like it weighed a hundred pounds. I hadn't actually weighed it before we left. I was afraid to. I'd jammed it full of all sorts of things.

Mark was carrying the tent that he and I would sleep in. Ruth had her own one-person tent, the kind that spreads out along the ground and makes it easier to keep your body heat inside.

They let me lead once we got under way. It was an easy walk for the first part. The paths from here were

77

well marked. Once we got up into the highlands, we'd have to be a little more careful. But even there, the rangers did a good job of keeping the paths in good shape.

Every time I set foot on one of these trails, it still amazed me that they were the only paths that crossed the High Sierras. How in the world had people managed to keep roads from being built? I couldn't figure it.

None of us talked as we hiked along. It was too nice a day for that. We all spent the time just moving along the trail, looking around only when we stopped to catch our breath.

We didn't drink the water from the cool mountain streams along the way. Oh, I probably would, in a pinch. But Mark said the streams now carried a wicked strain of virus that made you really sick. People got it all the time. To be safe, you had to boil any water you got from it.

It seemed strange to me that you had to boil water from a natural stream out in the wilderness. But Mark insisted it was true. There had been so many hikers, they'd brought the virus with them. The animals had caught it, and it now ran off into the streams in a lot of places.

I kept one eye out for the eagles the entire time we walked. I didn't really expect to see them until we got close to Cascade, but you never knew.

We took a break for lunch in the middle of the afternoon, after we'd walked close to three hours. The sun was no longer directly overhead. I thought that maybe we wouldn't get to the start of our climb before it got dark, but Ruth told me not to worry.

We were climbing steadily as we went along. It was

gradual, but I could really feel it in my legs. We'd started the climb at about 6,000 feet at the trailhead. We'd been moving up ever since. We'd wind up at just over 10,000 feet before we actually had to do hand-to-hand climbing up the rock face.

The trail worked its way back and forth up the mountainside. I counted at least a dozen switchbacks. I sometimes wondered why they just didn't have paths that went straight up to the top of mountains. Ruth said it was because the paths wouldn't last, and people couldn't climb up them. Too steep, she said.

The pines got smaller and sparser and then disappeared once we got close to 9,000 feet. There were more shrubs. Then, at 10,000 feet or so, even the stumpy pines vanished. Only the shrubs remained. And finally those disappeared as well.

The entire time we were climbing, I was only able to see the uppermost part of the Cascade peak. Ruth was right. It was almost entirely hidden by a separate ridge that made it nearly inaccessible by foot. You would have to go up and over an extra ridge to get to it, and who wanted to do that? There was no path that led directly to it.

The path we were on crossed through a wide pass, around to the eastern side of the mountain and then beyond. That was where we would make our climb: on the eastern slope.

We stopped, though, and had a brief snack before we moved into the pass. The sun was just starting to dip into the treeline to the west. We'd been hiking for about six hours, and it would be dark within two hours.

Now that we were up high, I kept my eyes riveted on the part of the Cascade peak I could see. Still no eagles. I looked down the length of the mountain, toward the valley. You could see a long way from where we were. It was quite a view.

"There they are," Ruth said softly.

I looked up sharply. I'd only taken my eyes from the peak for an instant, but that was all it took.

One of the eagles had left the eyrie. It was now working its way up to catch the winds that nearly always swirled high above the valley. A few seconds later, a second eagle took off.

I saw the spot where the second eagle left from. It seemed to be from a point about fifty feet below the absolute peak of the mountain, along a sheltered ridge. It had to be the eagles' eyrie.

We watched the eagles soar for about fifteen minutes. They stayed above the western slope of Cascade Mountain the entire time.

I kept waiting for one of two things to happen—the sharp report of a scope rifle, or for one of the eagles to drop from the sky to catch some prey. Neither happened. But I wasn't disappointed. It was fun just to watch them.

"Come on," Mark said finally. "We need to get moving if we want to set up camp before it's too dark to see."

We all got up and stretched our legs. I was stiff. I knew I'd be a little sore tomorrow. But I'd get over it quickly.

I stole a last glance at the eagles circling in the sky before we moved into the pass and lost sight of the western slope. The babies had never come out of the nest.

It took us another hour to get to the rock face. It was deep dusk by the time we started to set up our camp. But Mark and Ruth were fast. They had the tent up and dinner ready by the time it got dark. With the little glow lamp Ruth had brought, we could see just about everything we needed.

Dinner consisted of hard biscuits, jerky, and some dried fruit. It was OK. Not exactly a gourmet meal, but everything tasted good right now.

"You know," Ruth said toward the end of dinner, "they say John Muir used to just stuff a whole bunch of hard biscuits in the pockets of an oversized coat before he set off into the Sierras."

Mark nodded. "Yeah, I've heard that, too."

"Once he'd run out of biscuits, he lived off the land," Ruth added.

"Who, exactly, was John Muir?" I finally worked up the courage to ask. I'd heard of him, of course. He was kind of a legend in the High Sierras. I heard about him all over the place, but I didn't actually know who he was.

"Come on. You know who he was, don't you?" Ruth teased.

"Well, yeah, kinda. But I don't know all that much about him," I said defensively.

"He was one of the first people to seriously hike through all these parts, around the turn of the century," Mark said.

"I know that." I frowned. "But, I mean, like who *was* he, really? And why do people talk about him so much?"

Ruth looked over at Mark. She took a stab at it. "It's more than the fact that he hiked through here so much. Lots of people do that. It's that he actually did more than that."

"Like what?" I pressed.

81

"Like fight with congress and presidents to do something to keep the Sierras from becoming buried with superhighways and cities and smog and things like that," Ruth said.

"How'd he do that?"

"Well, for one, he fought like crazy to make sure there were national parks like Yosemite out here, which has gone a long way toward making sure that things stay pretty much the way they were back then," Mark offered.

"Is that why there aren't any roads through the Sierras?" I asked.

"Partly," Mark said. "And partly because John Muir started something, and other people got involved, and pretty soon there were even more people fighting to keep at least one part of our wilderness in the West the way it was once."

"So what did he start?" I asked. This was all so new to me. I'd never really thought about it before. There were mountains and streams and pine trees and big boulders and animals and that was pretty much the way it was. That was the way it always *had* been. It had never occurred to me that you actually had to fight to keep it that way.

"He started a movement," Ruth said. She leaned forward, toward the little glow light that was all that stood between us and the darkness. Ruth's face was really animated by the funny little light. "Sort of a movement to save the earth."

"The environmental movement," Mark added.

"But doesn't, like, everyone want to save the earth?" I said.

"Sure. I guess." Ruth was really into this now. This was her thing, what she lived and breathed for. "But

John Muir went way beyond that. He actually did something. He didn't just talk about it."

I glanced over at Mark, who wasn't in his National Park Service uniform right now. But he was still a ranger. "Kind of like what you do?" I asked him.

Mark shrugged. "Nobody paid John Muir to do what he did. He fought for the national parks and for the Sierras because he loved them. It was his duty, he felt, and he did it for that reason. Nothing more."

"You'd work at this anyway." Ruth smiled warmly. "Right?"

"Got to support my family, though," Mark said.

Ruth leaned closer into the little light. "Something funny happened along the way, though. What John Muir started became something else entirely."

"What?" I asked.

Ruth glanced over at Mark. "You know what I'm talking about, don't you? You face it every day."

"Not every day, but, yeah, I know what you're talking about." I could see Mark was a little uncomfortable. He didn't usually talk about himself, or what he was feeling.

"So what is it, already?" I demanded.

Ruth glanced around at the darkness. "This. All around us. The earth. Nature. The wilderness. It's kind of replaced God to a whole bunch of people."

"Replaced God?"

"Taken His place. People worship nature. They worship the earth. They live their lives to serve the beauty of the creation."

"That's kind of strange, isn't it?" I asked softly.

"Yes, it is—*I* think," Ruth said forcefully. I could see that this was something she'd thought about. A lot. "Once, it was easy to love the earth and love God at the same time. It's not so easy now."

"Oh, come on," I said. "That doesn't make sense."

Mark spoke up. "She's right, Josh. The lines got real blurry at some point. Now, there's almost open hostility between people who call themselves environmentalists and those who call themselves Christians."

"Which is really strange, when you think about it," Ruth continued, "because, once, people like John Muir believed in God but still loved nature and felt like it was their duty to protect and preserve nature without worshiping it."

"It's easy, when you're out here, to get close to God," Mark said. "There isn't much of a buffer between you and Him. Not out here, there isn't."

"Is that why Jesus went into the wilderness for forty days?" I asked.

"Yes, exactly." Mark nodded. "I can't think of anywhere else on earth than right here to spend time trying to hear the still, small voice that people like Abraham, Moses, and others have heard down through the ages."

Nobody said anything for a long time. A certain stillness settled around us. It wasn't that it was quiet. It wasn't. There were sounds everywhere—crickets, wind, rustling leaves, hooting owls, other creatures of the night. But the calm was there anyway.

I could almost imagine what it had been like when John Muir walked these same regions. It hadn't changed much in a hundred years. Many of the same paths were still around. The mountains certainly hadn't changed. The same redwoods were still alive.

It made you feel very small, in the middle of all this grandeur. But the bigness of it all also made me feel like I was part of something quite vast and important at the same time.

The creation. I was part of it. But, maybe, like John Muir, I could do my part, too. Someday. You never knew.

"Daybreak," Ruth said when it was time to go to sleep. "We take the mountain at sunrise."

CHAPTER 13

△ I had no idea it was so cold in the mountains above 10,000 feet. It was *freezing*. My feet were blue and numb by morning. I was ready for a hot shower. There was no shower in sight, of course. And thinking about one made it worse.

"Aw, quit grumblin'," Ruth said. "It's not that cold. You'll be fine once you're up and moving and the sun's out."

"I don't know. I'm pretty miserable." I shook all over and pulled my windbreaker tighter around my neck. I blew on my hands and stamped my feet. Nothing helped.

I really wished we could start a fire. But they didn't allow that out in the wilderness. There was too great a risk of uncontrolled forest fires. So they didn't let you build any fires. Of course, people ignored that every so often. But I knew Mark, a ranger, would never do that just for the sake of warming some cold toes.

The rock face looked daunting this early in the morning. There were still shadows playing across the lower portion, where we'd be climbing first. The crevices looked deep. The handholds seemed few and far between.

But I was sure it would look easier once we were actually up on it. Everything always looked forbidding before you actually got there, I figured.

Ruth made certain that I had all my gear together, that my loops weren't ripping, that my shoes weren't too smooth on the soles. She checked the entire length of the rope to make sure there weren't any flaws.

"You always this careful?" I asked while she was running her hands along the core-filled nylon rope, checking for hidden cuts.

"You bet!" she said. "Always. I never make a climb until I've checked out every single inch of my equipment. It only takes one mistake. Just one."

Ruth decided to go a little slower than usual, because this was my first serious climb. We were going to stay fairly close together, even though this took longer. And both Mark and Ruth secured themselves while I climbed, just to be on the safe side.

"But you're treating me like I'm a big baby," I complained.

"No, we aren't," Ruth said. "I just want to make sure. Don't worry. It'll go quickly."

"I can hold my weight," I countered.

"Josh. We'll do it the way Ruth says," Mark said firmly. "She's the team leader. Period. End of discussion."

I just nodded and decided to bide my time. Once we were under way and well up on the rocks, I figured I could try again.

Ruth was fast—real fast. She was up and locked in place almost before Mark was ready to go. She could find handholds faster than I could blink, practically. From there, holding herself suspended with one arm, she'd search either for a new toehold or handhold.

Mark wasn't nearly so fast, but he was pretty good. He couldn't hold himself with one arm as well as Ruth could, but he had a longer reach and he could scale faster once he'd found a place to hold on to.

Then there was me. I felt like I was moving in slow motion, compared to them. It always seemed like it took forever to find a place to hold on to. And my foot always seemed to slip off a rock the first time I tried to step onto it.

"Don't rush," Ruth called down to me.

"I'm *not*," I muttered angrily.

Once I got the hang of the face, though, I got better. It grew easier to find small crevices to slip my fingers into, or jagged rocks I could cling to. I could tell by the lines of the rocks where I was likely to find openings. Plus, I used the time I was waiting for them to plan how I was going to climb.

My eye started to get better at judging distances to small outcroppings where I could plant a foot, or openings in the rock I could aim for where I could lock in place more easily.

Before I knew it, we were up several hundred feet. And the summit no longer seemed so impossibly high.

By mid-morning, I was ready for a break. Ruth could see that I needed to stop—if only for a few minutes— so she called a halt, locked herself into place securely, and waited for Mark and me to join her.

Once we three were all together, Ruth threw a second loop of rope around me, just to be on the safe side.

We pulled some juice and candy bars from our daypacks we were taking up with us. The bigger packs were still down on the ground with our tents.

We were high enough now that we had a clear view of the canyon that was carved out to the east of Cascade Mountain. It was a fairly wide canyon, with a large stream running down the center.

There were ridges on either side, extending out as far as the eye could see. You could get to the canyon more easily from the north than you could from the direction we'd come. There was a nearly straight path through a lower pass into the canyon. Pack trains came through there a lot, traveling south along the Great Western Divide.

I thought I'd spotted a thin curl of smoke coming from somewhere in the valley early that morning, which told me that someone was camping who didn't seem to have much regard for the law of the wilderness. I couldn't see the smoke anymore, but I was certain there were hikers down there.

I happened to glance up while I was drinking my juice, and I spotted the eagles. The adults were both out flying, this time to the east of their eyrie. They weren't up all that high, and I got a pretty good look at them.

They were huge. Their full wingspan had to be about seven feet, I figured. They were both circling together, almost in a pattern. They would kind of swirl around, up and down, like a dance. I was mesmerized.

The shots that rang out almost caused me to fall. *Crack! Crack! Crack!* Three of them, right in a row. Then there were two more shots, for a total of five in all.

"No!" I yelled, grabbing my ropes for safety. I looked up wildly, expecting the worst. I saw it.

The eagles had been hit, both of them. One of them was trying, vainly, to stay aloft. Just one wing was flapping and it was only a question of time before the hunters took it out of the sky before it could get to safety.

The other was falling like a stone. It had been hit and killed immediately. I watched it fall and then disappear into the sea of pines far below. Without thinking, I burst into tears. I started to bawl like a baby.

There were two more shots. The second eagle started to fall. Within seconds, it had joined its mate, disappearing into the pines far, far below.

Just like that, they were gone. A horrible, wrenching anger swept through me. It was so unfair! The eagles had been harming no one! Why would someone kill them for no reason at all?

I looked over at Ruth and Mark. I could barely make them out through my tear-filled eyes. Both of them were dumbstruck by what they'd just witnessed.

Ruth was the first to speak. "Oh, my," she managed, her voice filled with the horror I so clearly felt.

"They have no right," Mark said angrily, his voice cracking with emotion.

"You have to do something!" I cried out to him.

Mark looked over at me. I could see the deep anger in his eyes. But I could also sense the helplessness. "What can I do, Josh? I can't go arrest them. Not from here. And I can't bring those eagles back."

"But it's not right," I said, trying to stop the steady flow of tears. "They weren't hurting anything."

"It doesn't matter," Mark said grimly. "Somebody

91

was bound and determined to kill those eagles. For whatever reason."

We all felt the instant loss of something we'd only seen from a distance. But those eagles had been around for a while. People in Jupiter said they'd lived here, on Cascade Mountain, for nearly as long as anyone could remember. Even the Checkers Gang.

I would never forget the sight of first one and then the other eagle falling like a stone from the sky. Only a moment before, they'd been riding the air currents so majestically, their vast wings outstretched. And then . . . in the blink of an eye . . . they were gone. It wasn't right.

Then I remembered. "The babies!" I yelled almost at the top of my lungs. "There are baby eagles in the eyrie."

Ruth looked at me with sorrowful eyes. "I'm sorry, Josh."

"We have to get them!" I said. "We have to. They won't make it otherwise."

"Josh," Mark said gently. "We can't do that. They'll just have to fend for themselves. They have a chance. They're nearly old enough. They've probably been hunting on their own for a few weeks, by now."

I remembered that day when Ashley and I had been out hiking, when we'd seen the entire family of eagles out together. It hadn't looked to me that the babies knew yet how to fend for themselves. They'd stayed awfully close to their parents.

"They can't, Mark," I groaned. "I've seen them. They won't go out without their parents close by."

"They'll have to—now," Ruth said.

"They have no choice," added Mark.

I'd read enough about eagles to know that, in fact,

babies would stay put in their nests, crying for their parents, until they were weak and starved. Only then would they venture forth, and then it was usually too late. Miss Lily had said so too.

I just knew the same thing would happen here. Unless someone did something. Unless *we* did something.

"We've got to try," I pleaded. "Please? Can't we go climb up there? Force them to leave the nest before it's too late?"

Mark and Ruth looked at each other. I could see what they were thinking. They didn't have to say it. I knew.

"Josh, we just can't," Mark said. "It would take us at least a day to get there, and another day—or more— to climb to the eyrie. We can't do it."

"We could too," I said, fighting back the tears again. "We could! If you'd just try."

"Josh!" Mark said more sharply. "We can't do it, and that's final."

"But—"

"I mean it!" Mark said, his voice booming in the still air. "Now, that's enough!"

I glared at him. "You're not Mom. You can't order me around."

I hadn't tried that on him in months. I could see that it was like a punch to the solar plexus. Mark took a deep breath before responding to me. "I know you don't mean that, Josh."

"I do too," I said, letting my emotions get the better of me. I didn't *really* mean it. But the words just sort of came out, before I could bring them back. Now that they were out there, I just kept going.

"Josh, Mark's right," Ruth tried to calm me down.

"We can't really go get those baby eagles, even if we wanted to."

"Why not?" I demanded. "Why couldn't we make that climb?"

"Because we didn't come prepared for it," Ruth explained. "It's a much more difficult climb. I would want to take precautions. I haven't done that. It isn't safe."

"You're just saying that because you don't want to try," I said bitterly. "We could do it if you wanted. I know we could."

"That's the end of it, Josh," Mark said, looking me straight in the eye. "I'm very, very sorry those eagles were shot. I promise you I will do everything in my power to bring those hunters to justice, once we've returned. I give you my word. But we cannot make an attempt to go after those babies. I mean it."

I kept silent. I could see that there was no way I was going to change their minds, no way at all.

I could feel myself making a decision. Try as I might, I couldn't keep myself from thinking about it. I knew it was wrong. Deeply, terribly wrong. I would be breaking one of God's Ten Commandments, even if Mark was only my stepfather.

But I couldn't keep the thought from returning. An image of those two helpless baby eagles, crying for their now-dead parents, kept coming to mind.

I had to do something. I just had to, no matter if I was grounded until I got out of high school.

Which I would be. No doubt about it. If I disobeyed Mark and tried this, then it was much, much worse than anything I'd ever done. No two-weeks-of-staying-in-my-room on this one. It would be a far greater punishment.

Yet I knew, in my heart, that I was willing to risk it. No matter what the consequences, I was going to try to save those eagles. The thought was there, no matter where I turned.

"God, forgive me," I prayed silently. "Please. Please. Please. Forgive me."

△

CHAPTER 14

△ We climbed in silence for much of the rest of the afternoon. The death of the eagles had cast a pall over our trip. There was no mistaking it.

Once, there were eagles everywhere, just like there were buffalo and wolves and cougars and all sorts of creatures in the West. Then the settlers showed up, and the animals had been losing ground ever since.

When we reached the summit, I almost had no desire to look out over the valleys to the east. It was a breathtaking view. But it wasn't one I could enjoy. Not right now.

I could still imagine those baby eagles, raising a ruckus in the eyrie, wondering when they were going to receive their dinner.

We had a mid-afternoon snack at the top, and then made the descent. It was a lot quicker going down.

Ruth went last this time, and gathered up the equipment as we worked our way down the rock face.

I was concentrating so much on what I planned to do next, I was lucky I didn't fall and break my neck.

It was starting to get dark by the time we got to the ground. I should have been ecstatic, overwhelmed—my first real climb. But there was no joy, not for any of us.

Dinner was hard biscuits and jerky again. Mark broke out an extra candy bar he'd brought along. I ate my dinner mostly in silence, but I was grateful for the candy bar.

The valley was purple and orange and red as the sun set over the mountains to the west. So many of the leaves were changing colors, it was an amazing sight.

A chill northerly wind had rolled in while we'd been scaling the rock face. It would be colder tonight than it had been the night before. It definitely had a bite to it, just to remind us that we were moving closer to fall.

We went to bed early, just after the sun had set. We all packed before we went to sleep. Ruth wanted to get off early, first thing in the morning.

I waited until I was certain that Mark was asleep before I made my move. I always carried a small notebook and pen with me on trips like this, so I could keep a journal. I almost never wrote anything down, but I always liked having it with me.

It came in handy now. I wrote Mark a quick note and attached it to the zipper on the inside of the tent, where he was sure to see it:

Mark, I couldn't stand the thought of staying up here, where the eagles were, any longer. I got an early start down the mountain. I'll meet you along the trail. Josh.

It was a bald-faced lie. But it was tame compared to what I was about to do. The note would send them on a wild-goose chase down the mountain.

I would be long gone, meanwhile. I was crossing through the Cascade pass tonight, and I was going to work my way through and over the ridge as much as I could before setting up camp. I'd make the ascent to rescue the baby eagles sometime in the afternoon, I figured.

I had no tent for a shelter, but I did have a tarp, which I could stake to the ground and use as a lean-to. It would have to do. I had no other choice.

I'd brought the equipment with me for a solo climb. I can't say why I did. A hunch, I guess. But one that had come through. I'd also taken Ruth's extra-long nylon rope, with the solid core, so that I'd have enough rope with me to tie to pitons all the way up.

I had no idea how hard it would actually be to climb to the eagles' eyrie. But I didn't care how hard it would be. I was going to do it. I'd made up my mind, and that was that.

I gathered up my sleeping gear and my backpack and stole away into the night as silently as I could. Mark didn't even stir. Ruth's tent was quiet as I slipped away from the camp.

I felt absolutely, completely rotten about what I was doing. I knew that Mark would go crazy when he didn't find me. He'd have a terrible day wondering what had happened to me.

But the way I had it figured, I had to trick him to keep him from coming after me and stopping me from climbing up to the eagles. It was the only thing I could think of.

If all went well, I would find them by the second day out, before he'd gone completely out of his mind wondering what had happened to me. *If* all went well.

It was quite cool when I set off, enough so that I had to wear my windbreaker on the path. It was easy going, thanks to a half-moon and a night chock-full of stars.

That was one of the first things I noticed soon after I'd moved here from Washington, D.C. You could see ten times as many stars here as you could in the D.C. suburbs. In fact, on some nights, it was very bright out at night. And tonight was one of those times.

I had no trouble at all through the pass. I started a little when a coyote bayed at the moon, but there was no other trouble.

Once through the pass, I made a hard left straight into the woods. I used my compass to guide me toward the crest of the ridge. It wasn't like there were road signs out here to let you know that you were going where you wanted to go.

I had to go up and over a ridge, down into an alpine meadow or forest—I wouldn't know until I got there—and then back up another fairly steep ridge to get to the rock face. It wouldn't be easy to do in the semi-darkness. I'd have to trust my instincts and my compass.

I trudged along in the darkness for what seemed like an eternity, constantly working my way up. I knew I had to be going in the right direction because everything ran up to the first ridge. I might be drifting away from the rock face to the north, but at least I was going up.

I reached the crest probably an hour or two before dawn. I'd scared a few squirrels, chased a few birds away, roused a possum or skunk—I couldn't tell which in the dark—and stumbled on a doe and her fawn. They bounded away from me in terror.

But I didn't run across any cougars or bears, for which I was very grateful. I'm not sure what I would have done had I come across either.

I worked my way down the other side of the ridge. I was bone tired, and all I wanted to do was drop to the ground and sleep. But I pushed on as much as I could possibly manage.

After a while, every pine tree became a blur. Every shrub became identical. I had no idea where I was in relation to the eyrie, but I no longer cared. I just wanted to get to level ground so I could sleep. It made no difference where.

Just as the first streaks of light began to appear over the horizon, I finally arrived at a clearing of sorts where it was level enough to set up my lean-to.

I fumbled around in the dawn light. It took me forever to get the lean-to in place, but at last I managed it. I threw my sleeping bag on the ground, and I was asleep almost the moment my head hit the ground.

△
CHAPTER 15

△ I bolted upright, and promptly banged my head against one of the sticks that held my tarp in place. My back was roasting. The sun had been up for hours, and it was now beating down on my tarp, heating it up. It had to be mid-morning.

My heart raced. I was completely disoriented. Where was I? How had I come to be here? Where was Mark?

Then I remembered. My body ached from the trip through the dark woods. My feet were sore. I had a pounding headache. But I had made it this far. Now the hard part began.

I reached in my backpack and pulled out the last of my hard biscuits. I wolfed them down, and then washed them down with part of the water I had left. I saved some for after my trip up the rock face to the eagles' eyrie.

I hesitated with the jerky. I had half a dozen strips left. I wanted to save at least two each for the eagles, to lure them away from the nest. But I decided that it was better to have my strength for the climb, and ate the two remaining pieces I'd saved for myself.

I now had no food—except for the jerky I was saving for the eagles—and almost no water. I was out in the middle of the wilderness, about to climb a rock face—solo—to the top of a 12,000-foot mountain to rescue two baby eagles.

I started laughing out loud. It seemed crazy. Had someone told me at the start of the summer that I'd be doing something like this by the end of the summer, I'd have told them to go take a hike.

But it didn't really seem so crazy now. I'd learned the wilderness. It no longer filled me with terror the way it had when we'd first moved to the Sierra Nevadas. I felt like I knew my way around. I knew what the different parts of the forests and mountains meant. I knew where animals were, and what they did.

The climbing part, that was different. This, I knew, I should not be doing by myself. But I really did feel like I could do this. I'd studied it and practiced. Now I just had to do it.

I'd brought plenty of pitons and carabiners, plus I now had nearly three hundred feet of rope—the length of a football field. That should be enough, I figured.

I'd thought about bringing wedges to use instead of pitons, but had decided against it. Hard-core climbers who don't like to drive pitons into rock will use wedges instead. They look for cracks and slip the wedges in, run the rope through the carabiners, and

104

then go on their way. That way, they don't put holes in the rock.

But pitons were a whole lot safer for someone like me. I could drive the pitons in and then use them to stand on if I couldn't find footholds. Plus, I didn't have to look for cracks or crevices. It would be a little slower going, but infinitely safer.

I was going to drive the pitons into the wall as I went along, and then leave them in place. There was a rope looped through the end of the pitons, and then the oval-shaped carabiners with the inward-breaking latch on the end of that rope. I would run my safety rope through the carabiner.

If all went well, then there would be a series of pitons going up the wall. Once I got to the eyrie, and got the eagles, then I was going to climb very slowly back down the cliff. I'd already decided to just leave the pitons in place.

With the eagles safely tucked in my smaller daypack—assuming I could actually get them into the pack—it would be too hard to "down climb" and re-move the pitons. I'd just have to leave them in place. Maybe another climber, someday, could remove them.

I peeked out of my lean-to and looked around. I couldn't see anything, really, because there were pine trees and a few scattered redwoods everywhere. I thought I could see the cliff face through the trees, off in the distance, but I couldn't be certain.

I folded the tarp up quickly, jammed it in my backpack, and got moving. I had no time to waste now. I had to find the cliff face by lunch time if I had any hope of getting up to the eagles' eyrie and back down before it got dark that evening.

I shuddered. What would I do if I was stuck on the

cliff when it got dark? The prospect terrified me. But I'd deal with that problem if it came up. No time to worry about it now.

It was a glorious, crisp morning, with a slight chill in the air. I was surprised that I hadn't frozen during the night. But then, I'd gone to sleep right before dawn, just when the chill begins to wear off. I'd slept until the sun was up and had begun to warm the air.

There were noises and creatures everywhere. Some black ravens went cawing off into the trees nearby. I stumbled on patches of bumblebees three times. Squirrels were busily gathering as many pine nuts as they could.

I worked my way up the second ridge, which really wasn't a ridge but the ascent to the mountaintop itself. As I walked uphill, the trees began to thin. I still had no idea if I was close to the eyrie or not.

I stopped. My body went cold, and the bottom dropped out of my stomach. I had no idea where to begin my climb. The cliff face wasn't marked. There was no way to spot the eyrie from the ground. How would I know if I'd gotten to the right place?

There could be a dozen cliff faces on this side, any of which might or might not lead up to the eyrie. I'd have to be absolutely certain before I began my climb. If I guessed wrong, I could wind up at a summit with no hope of getting to the eagles.

I stood there in the forest of trees for a very long time, puzzling it all out. I had no hope of finding an answer. There was no way. It was hopeless.

But maybe not. I'd often thought about moments like this, when you needed help and there was no help to be found. What did you do then? The only thing you could, really.

"God," I said out loud. "I need help. I know what I'm doing is wrong. I know that. And I'm sorry. Please forgive me. Please help me now. Please. I won't make it if You don't help."

I'm not sure why I said it out loud. It wasn't like there was anyone around to hear me. But I felt better now. Not so scared. Not so uncertain. I felt like I had a friend, an ally. God would help. I just knew it.

I decided to keep heading upward until I got to the closest cliff face. I'd figure out what to do next once I'd gotten there.

As I climbed, the trees started thinning rapidly. After an hour, they'd grown sparse enough that I could see almost a hundred feet or so in front of me. The landscape was changing dramatically. There were more shrubs, less undergrowth, and more big boulders.

When the sun was almost directly overhead, I caught my first real glimpse of the cliff before me. I saw the grayish rock through the trees, and I almost broke out into a run. But I didn't. I had to conserve my energy.

As I walked, I began to look back and forth in both directions, hoping for some sign of where I was and which direction I should go. But there was nothing special or unusual about either direction. Gray rock loomed on either side.

I came to the edge of the treeline and stopped. To my left, the cliff face ran as far as the eye could see until it disappeared down a slope. To my right, the cliff ran up a little and then receded around a turn.

I turned around and looked behind me. There was no help there. The trees blocked any kind of a view from where I stood.

I decided to go to the right. I could always back-track. It was easy to walk here. I just had to pick my way through the boulders.

As I started walking along the cliff face, I looked up expectantly every so often. I wasn't sure what I was looking for. A sign, I guess. Something that would tell me where the eagles were.

It was a whole lot quieter here. About the only thing I heard was the wind whipping around the rocks. There was no growth here. Just rocks and boulders. This was the alpine level, and not much grew here.

By now, Mark and Ruth would be well down the path. They wouldn't find out I hadn't made it until they got to the car at the end of the day. Then, Mark would go into a panic. He'd probably radio into the ranger station, and they'd call out the whole world to come find me.

I hurried my pace. I had to get to those eagles by this afternoon, or I'd never get there. There were two helicopters at a forest ranger station about thirty miles away, and I was sure Mark would call them in.

I wasn't exactly sure what I'd do if I spotted one of the helicopters. Would I hide, or would I let them know where I was so they'd know I was safe? If I signaled to the helicopters, and I hadn't found the eagles yet, then it was all over. They'd land and get me. Simple as that. So I'd probably hide from them, if I could.

I walked for about half an hour, with no sign or clue. The rocks were all the same. The cliff was the same everywhere. There was no way to tell any of it apart.

Finally, in total frustration, I stopped and sat down, with my back against the cliff. I was already tired, and I hadn't even begun to climb yet.

I reached into my backpack and rummaged around, just to make sure I hadn't overlooked any food. Nothing. Except for the jerky I was saving, I was out of food. There was absolutely nothing to eat in there. I pulled the water bottle out and finished off the last of my water.

I leaned my head back against the rock, which was warm from the sun's rays, and closed my eyes. I sat there for the longest time, just listening to the wind. I let the sun beat down on my face.

Where was my sign? I thought. *Were the eagles nearby? Have I gone too far? In the wrong direction?*

I looked up. It all looked so much alike. There was really no way to tell if I was close at all.

It occurred to me that I had no right to ask God to help with this quest. I was disobeying my stepfather and doing something I absolutely should not be doing. So why should He help me?

"All right!" I yelled to no one in particular. "I'm just gonna climb, then."

It was crazy, I knew. But this was as good a spot as any to try. If this didn't work, then perhaps I could try another. Perhaps, but not likely.

△
CHAPTER 16

△ I estimated that it was about a hundred and fifty feet to the summit, so it was possible I could make the climb with just one rope. But I took a second rope, just in case. I also took as many pitons as I could carry, a sling, and my daypack.

I was already starting to get hungry, and I was sure the eagles—if I found them—would be hungry as well. I was tempted to eat the remaining jerky. But I didn't. I wanted to save it.

After securely anchoring my rope to a jagged out-cropping at the base of the cliff, I took a few minutes to plan my ascent. I chose a route, finally, that had a few easy handholds at the beginning. I wanted to get the hang of this before I got well up on the wall.

It was much, much more difficult than I'd imag-ined. Solo climbing wasn't anything like climbing with a partner—especially one like Ruth, who knew exactly what she was doing.

111

I'd gotten used to the way Ruth always held the slack rope and kept an eye on me as I climbed. I never had to worry about play in the rope or anything like that.

Here, though, I had to worry about everything myself. I had to watch the rope myself, and make sure I was hammering the pitons deep enough. Plus, I had to hold onto the wall or stand on a piton as I fumbled around for my hammer or another piton.

I did have a special latch for solo climbing attached to my harness belt, though I'd never used it much before. As I climbed, the rope anchored below would feed through it, but it locked from the opposite direction: If I fell, the latch would "bite" the rope, keeping me from falling farther.

After half a dozen tries, I finally got the hang of it. Letting the rope hang over my shoulder, I'd flatten out against the wall, holding on with one hand. Balancing on the previous piton I'd driven into the wall, I'd reach into my piton bag with my free hand, grab one, and then jam it hard into an opening in the cliff face so that it didn't fall. If there wasn't an opening, I'd chip one with my hammer.

Then, I'd grab my hammer, aim carefully, and give it a good *whack*. I'd missed once, and the piton had jumped loose and fallen to the ground. When the piton was hammered into place, I'd attach the carabiner and then slide the coiled rope into it. The latch on the carabiner was spring-loaded and made a comforting sound as it snapped solidly closed. I'd grab the piton and move on.

It seemed to be working. It took me nearly an hour to climb just thirty feet, but I knew that the next thirty feet would go faster. I was getting a lot better at it as I went along.

The sun was really starting to beat down. Even though it was the end of the summer, and the nights were getting quite cold, the afternoons were still plenty hot. I was drenched with sweat.

I wished I'd remembered to borrow Ruth's chalk bag. She always carried one, to make sure sweat never made her hands too slick. I'd never liked the chalk bag because my hands never got all sweaty. But I was reconsidering, now that I was up here by myself. Fear did funny things to your palms.

I wanted to get to the top as quickly as I could, and I didn't want to take time even to look around. I only risked looking out over my shoulder one time, and the one look didn't help much. All I could see was the top of the ridge I'd crossed during the night, and it was just a steady, unbroken sea of trees. Nothing jumped out at me.

I kept climbing. I got into a rhythm: Reach, hold, flatten, grab a piton, slam, reach for my hammer, hit the piton, drive it into the wall, then climb again.

I found that it was getting easier to find handholds that could get me up to a point where I could stand on the piton I'd just driven into the rock. It gave me something to aim for.

With pitons driven into the wall about every five feet or so, I felt relatively safe on the cliff face. If I fell, then I would only fall just below the last piton I'd driven in, plus the play in the rope attached to my belt loop. Even if one or two of the pitons were ripped loose, I still had all the other pitons in place.

There were almost no sounds up here, except the wind. I kept expecting to hear something, anything.

Some sign of life other than my labored breathing. But I heard nothing. I was alone.

The hours slipped by. I kept climbing. My hands were starting to ache terribly from the effort. My legs were cramping a little. I desperately wanted a cool drink of water. But I pressed on, and put any thought of water out of my mind.

It was the shadows on the wall that finally made me start to panic. I glanced down, once, and I spotted them. The sun was starting to dip behind the mountains to the west! I looked up in terror. I still had a ways to go to get to the summit.

Then I came to the end of my 150-foot rope and I had to pull out the reserve. I tied the two ropes together quickly and speeded up. I wasn't sure I'd make it to the summit before nightfall.

I tried to push it harder, faster. I drove pitons faster. I looked for handholds quickly. I didn't waste any time.

I was starting to get careless, cut corners. But I felt like I had to risk it. I was starting to run out of time.

I spotted a line to a crevice. I decided to risk climbing without pitons for about ten to fifteen feet, to get to the crevice. I knew I could do it. I could see the line clearly. Four handholds, and I was there.

But the third proved to be just out of my reach. I stretched out as far as I could. I was still a few inches away. I reached just a little farther . . .

My foot slipped. *"Aaaggghhh!"* I screamed. I clawed at the cliff face. My other foot hit the wall, propelling me out. I started to fall. My body tilted slightly backward as I fell.

Instinctively, I pulled my head in toward my body. If I was flat out when the rope jerked, it could break my back. That was one of the first things Ruth taught me. You had to know how to fall.

It seemed like it took forever. All kinds of thoughts flashed through my mind at the same time. Would the latch on my harness belt hold? Would the two ropes tied together hold? Would the rope remain anchored? Were the pitons OK?

There was a vicious jerk as the rope stretched out, then tugged hard on the last piton. I slammed into the wall. The harness latch held, the rope caught at my belt, and the rest of the rope did its job. But the piton ripped loose, and I fell again.

The second piton ripped free as well, and I fell another five feet or so. The free rope I was holding fell and cascaded down the side of the cliff. But the third piton held. I was fifteen feet below it, and my body hurt all over from the fall. But I was OK. Nothing was broken, and all the rest of my pitons had held.

My heart was racing furiously. My head was pounding. Adrenaline surged through my body. I'd gone too fast. I'd taken too many risks I shouldn't have taken. And I'd almost paid for it dearly.

"Ohhhhh," I groaned, holding my head. The helmet had helped when I'd slammed into the wall, but I'd still have a splitting headache. No question about it.

Slowly, painfully, I pulled myself into a climbing position. I gathered up the uncoiled rope and then walked back up the wall. It all took a very long time. I kept my eyes riveted on the remaining pitons to make sure none were pulling free of the rock.

I was losing valuable time, but I didn't care. I wasn't going to hurry again, even if I was stranded. I had to do it the right way, the safe way. I had no choice. Not now. I was too scared.

Every part of me was shaking. I could barely control my muscles I was so frightened. The fall had terrified me. I'd fallen before, even farther than I had here. But never alone. Never on a rock face like this, with no one there to brace my fall.

I knew—now—that what I'd done was terribly, terribly wrong. I shouldn't be here. It wasn't right. I should never have tried this, no matter how much I wanted to save those eagles.

I started to cry. The tears just came gushing out, staining my dirty cheeks and dribbling to the ground. I felt so awfully, terribly alone.

I'm so sorry, God, I prayed silently. *Please forgive me. Help me, even though I don't deserve it.*

Mom had always taught me that Jesus said those who asked for forgiveness and brought their troubles to Him would be forgiven. I hoped so. What I had done was so wrong that I had no hope of ever being forgiven otherwise.

I remembered a story Mom had told me once, about how when Jesus was out in the wilderness, Satan had tried to tempt Him. He'd encouraged Him to jump from the pinnacle of the temple in Jerusalem because God's angels would keep Him from falling.

"If You are the Son of God, throw Yourself down from here," Satan told Jesus. "For it is written: 'He shall give His angels charge over You, to keep You.' "

But Jesus refused, and told Satan, "It has been said, 'You shall not tempt the Lord your God.' "

Had I tempted God? I didn't know. I hadn't meant to. All I'd wanted to do was find and help the eagles. That was all. Nothing more. But I *felt* like I'd tempted God. I felt like I'd crossed over the line, and now everything was going crazy on me.

116

Slowly, deliberately, I returned to the last piton. I held onto it for all I was worth. I couldn't go on. I couldn't go down. I was paralyzed on the rock face. The sun was going down. I didn't know what to do. It would start to get dark within an hour, and I wouldn't be able to climb anymore.

I looked along the length of the rope that led down to the ground. It had taken me close to five hours to get this far, I figured. If I went down now, I would never make the climb back up again. Never. The eagles would die.

I didn't take long to make my decision. I was still terrified. But I had to press on. I *had* to. I couldn't quit. I'd gotten this far. I had to keep going.

I would climb until it started to get dark. Then I would set up the sling and spend the night on the cliff face. Other climbers had done it. Why couldn't I? Why not?

I took my time. No need to hurry now, not if I wasn't going to make it to the summit by nightfall. I was more careful about where I was reaching and stepping now. I was *very* careful.

I climbed for another half an hour or so. I was probably still a good hundred feet or so from the top of the cliff. It seemed like a mile. I didn't think I'd ever make it.

I stopped when the shadows had taken over the cliff, and the glow from the sun had disappeared to the west. It was still light enough to see, but I didn't want to risk another fall.

I hammered two pitons in, side by side, and then looped one end of the sling to them. Then I climbed to the side, hammered two more pitons in, and fastened the other end of the sling to them.

Gingerly, carefully, I climbed into the sling. It felt so strange, hanging out over the rocks like this. But it was also wonderful to be off my feet. Nearly every part of my body was in pain, as much from fear as from either the fall or the climb.

I knew I would never be able to get comfortable during the night. The only position that made any sense was to rest on my back, with one side pinned up against the cliff. I draped my arms in front of me and tried to rest.

But I couldn't rest. My mind continued to conjure up every possible nightmare. I was certain the pitons would slip free during the night. I figured the sling would rip or something.

The wind was whipping up. It was already starting to get cold. I hadn't brought my sleeping bag with me, obviously, so I would be very, very cold by morning. But there was no getting around that. I'd made my bed, so to speak, and now I was going to have to lie in it.

I reached up and peeked out over the edge of my sling. It was almost dark by now. Faintly, the sounds of night reached my ears. I could hear the crickets far, far below. It seemed such a long distance to them and the relative safety of the forest.

I wished now that I'd chosen to go back down and given up my quest to save the eagles. But it was too late—much, much too late. I had to go forward.

$\triangle$

CHAPTER 17

$\triangle$ Every little sound—every creaking tree limb, every hooting owl, every gust of wind whistling around the rocks, every howling coyote somewhere off in the distance—kept me awake. I waited for those sounds. I dreaded those sounds.

I felt as though I would drop like a stone at any moment. Every sound I heard made me realize I was suspended in midair, high above the earth. Those sounds were distant, yet close enough to let me know that I was part of them.

I wasn't an eagle. I had no right to be up here, sleeping where they slept. I was out of my mind. How had I come to this point? What had possessed me?

It was the longest conversation I'd ever had with God. At some point during the night, I had this feeling of incredible, shrinking smallness, like I was an inconsequential pinpoint in the middle of a huge, cavernous room. And I kept getting smaller.

Yet, even as I felt just how small I was, I could also sense that I was, still, somehow, important in the middle of it. I meant something. To Mom, to Mark, to Ashley, to Mr. Wilson, to Ruth. And, of course, to God.

For I could see quite clearly now my relationship to Him. I was small, yes, but I was somehow important to Him. He was everywhere all at once. Yet He kept track of me, listened to me, watched me, *cared* for me.

I can't say, really, when I crossed the divide. Not the Great Western Divide, where I was sleeping, but the divide between Him and me.

I was so sorry for what I'd done, for the pain and anguish I knew I was, even now, subjecting my parents to. And it was that pain that had separated me from God. I had done something terribly wrong. I would pay a price for it.

But I could feel, through the night, that God would forgive me. No, He had forgiven me already, before I'd even asked. I knew that, somehow. I just needed to get to the point where I believed it.

That's when I crossed—with a leap of faith. It was a little like standing at the edge of a canyon, believing you could jump to the other side, yet not knowing if, in fact, you could.

Then you leaped, not quite sure what awaited you— and you landed on the other side. Happy, joyous, relieved, not quite sure why you hadn't jumped before.

That's what I felt sometime in the middle of that deep, dark, silent night on the mountain. Relief and joy that God had, indeed, forgiven me for my awful sin against my parents.

It would be all right. It would work out in the end. I was as certain of that as I had been of anything in my life.

The sounds were gentle, a little distant. Yet clear enough that I recognized them. I drifted awake slowly.

I had no idea how long I'd been asleep. At some point, I'd grown too weary of holding myself awake. The terror of where I was, and what could happen to me, finally ebbed and I'd fallen asleep.

Yet those sounds. I'd heard them and awakened. I knew those sounds. Though I'd never heard them before, I'd read of them. I'd wondered about them. I was certain of what they were.

It sounded a little like kittens mewing—sharper and louder than that, but very much like kittens. But they weren't kittens. They were baby eagles, calling out desperately for their now-dead parents.

They were above me, and just a little to my right. God had given me His sign, after all. I would find them in the morning. I was certain of it now.

But I had not found them until I'd crossed that yawning gulf between the two of us, until I'd confessed my sin and asked for His forgiveness. Only then could He answer my prayer, and speak to my heart.

I fell asleep quickly this time, secure in the knowledge that I would find the eagles in the morning, that it would all somehow, miraculously, work out.

△
CHAPTER 18

△ I was so stiff the next morning that I could barely move. It had been raw, biting, nerve-tingling cold in the sling. I probably had pneumonia. I couldn't stop shivering. I'd never been this cold in my life. *Never.*

I could no longer hear the baby eagles. The sound of their call still echoed in my mind, though. It had not been a dream. I'd heard them. They were somewhere above me.

It took me about ten minutes to get clear of my sling. I didn't bother to try and fold it up. I let it hang where it was. I could either get it on the way down, or let it drop when I returned.

The sound of the eagles had been up and to my right, so I began to work my way in that direction. I went up, then sideways; then up, then sideways. I did that for nearly half an hour before returning to a straight ascent.

I wasn't sure, exactly, where I would find the eagles. I hoped they were accessible. But there was no way of knowing until I got there, of course.

I was bathed completely in shadow. The rock was ice-cold. My fingers were numb. I kept half expecting to simply lose my grip and fall. I could barely hang on to the rocks. I'd lost almost all feeling in my feet.

Yet I continued on. I had new hope, a new spirit, this morning. I could make it. I knew I could.

I kept expecting, at any minute, to hear the *whop-whop-whop* of an approaching helicopter. Mark would have radioed in by now, and they'd be out in force looking for me.

But it occurred to me that they would, most likely, be looking for me on the *other* side of the mountain, in the pines and woods leading to the valley on the other side. After all, that's where I'd been when I'd vanished. That was where they would logically look first.

Only later would they think to journey to the western side of Cascade Mountain. And even then, I had gone quite far south, well off the trail that led through the pass. Only a helicopter was likely to spot me.

By late morning, the end was in sight. I was sure I could see the summit. I also thought I heard the sound of a helicopter well off in the distance, but I couldn't be sure. It was on the other side of the mountain, and the sound didn't carry well.

Near the top, the cliff face started to angle out, away from the mountain. It was beginning to get very difficult to climb. I could no longer lie flat against the rock so easily.

Just as I was about to make a decision to go another direction, away from the inclining rock, I saw it.

Tucked into a very deep crevice, nearly at the top of the cliff, was the nest. It was huge, nearly five or six feet across, with grass sticking out in all directions.

It was also on the hardest possible part of the rock face to get to. The cliff angled out even more steeply at the point where the nest had been built.

I looked above the nest. There was absolutely no way at all to get to it from that angle, because the nest had been built under an overhanging rock. I'd have to go out over the overhang, and then drop down with a rope and swing into the nest. There was no way I was going to try anything like that.

No, I'd have to climb up to the nest, relying on my pitons and ropes to hold me secure. Once there, I had no idea at all how I was going to corral the eagles, other than to offer them the jerky I'd held on to. I'd deal with that when I got there.

I couldn't see if there were, in fact, any eagles in the nest—not from where I was right now. I listened, but I couldn't hear any sounds coming from it. I wasn't sure how I would feel if I got there and it was empty.

I moved sideways across the rock for almost half an hour to get into position. As I moved beneath the nest, I almost despaired. As I looked out, the nest was actually farther out from where I was by some five feet or so. I'd have to make the entire climb holding on to the pitons and crevices. I wouldn't be able to let go for even a moment.

Yet I was so close—I'd come so far—that I truly felt I could make it. I *would* make it. I had to.

I inched up the rock, carefully, cautiously, gripping the rocks and the pitons with every last ounce of my strength. I didn't dare look up because it meant leaning back slightly.

The sun started to peek over the top of the mountain. At the moment that the first rays hit the rocks, I heard the eagles. They'd seen the sun, too, and had reacted to it.

They sounded weak. Their voices croaked and mewed softly. Their parents had been killed on the afternoon of the previous day, so they probably hadn't eaten in a day and a half, maybe two days.

"Hang on," I whispered. "I'm coming."

I didn't think they'd heard me, but their mewing suddenly stopped. I had this eerie feeling that the eagles were now waiting for my arrival.

The nest had been built into a crevice. I was hoping that I'd be able to actually climb into the crevice. It was my only hope, really. I'd never be able to get them if I had to hold on to the rocks and go after them. I had to actually *be* in the nest, or close by, to have a shot.

Beads of sweat began to drip down my face as the sun edged out over the mountaintop, heating things up. It amazed me how I could have been so cold just a few hours earlier, and absolutely roasting now.

As I neared the nest, I was certain the eagles had heard me. They'd probably heard me from a long way off. After all, I made quite a racket when I pounded the pitons in.

When I got to within a few feet of the nest, they started to squawk and squeal loudly. I don't know who was more afraid—them or me. The din was unbelievable.

It looked impossible to come up to the nest on the left, so I climbed under the crevice and tried an approach from the right. It was easier going in that direction. There was a slight opening on the rock face, at the opening of the crevice.

I almost reached up with my hand and grabbed the crevice. At the last second, I thought better of it. Instead, I took my hammer, turned it around, and inched the handle up and over the edge.

A sharp beak reached out and tried to take a big *chomp* out of the handle. I thanked my lucky stars that it hadn't been my hand. I'd be bleeding profusely now if it had been.

I stuck the handle of the hammer up there several more times. The eagles tried to bite it every time.

This wasn't going to be easy, I could see that now. I wasn't sure why I'd ever thought I could manage this anyway. These baby eagles weren't exactly "babies" anymore. They were nearly full grown—immature and afraid to leave the nest, but still rather large.

I'd have to frighten them. I'd have to get them to back off to the opposite edge of the nest. I had no other choice.

I mapped my plan of attack. I'd have to secure two pitons right below the edge, tie a rope between them, bang my hammer hard, let out a war whoop to get them disoriented, and then sort of pull myself up and over the edge before they knew what hit them.

I felt a little like a soldier scaling an enemy wall. I had no idea what awaited me over the edge. I had no way of knowing until I got there. I pulled my daypack free and clipped it to my belt.

I suddenly remembered that I'd jammed a pair of gloves down at the bottom of my daypack before I'd left, just in case my hands got cold. Gloves! What a discovery! With gloves on my hands, the eagles' claws and beaks wouldn't hurt nearly as much. Frantically, I searched the pack. I breathed a sigh of relief when I spotted them.

If there were, in fact, two eagles there, I decided right then that I had to go for the closest one, and try to wrestle it into the pack. I wasn't sure what I'd do about the other one.

It seemed like it took me an hour to drive the pitons in and tie the rope between them. My hands were raw and aching terribly. I was weary beyond belief. I just wanted to collapse somewhere.

But at last I was ready to make the assault. I steeled myself, said one more quick prayer, and grabbed the rope.

The sudden *whop! whop!* of the helicopter screaming over the top of the mountain nearly knocked me from my perch. It had come out of nowhere. I'd been concentrating so hard on the nest, I hadn't heard its approach.

The helicopter roared past me and out over the forest and valley below me. I looked out, desperately hoping I could signal it.

"Hey! Over here! Over here! On the cliff! I'm over here!" I yelled at the top of my lungs. But my voice was drowned out by the roar of the helicopter. I kept calling, though, even knowing that it was hopeless. There was nothing else to be done.

I couldn't even signal to it. I was hidden from the sky by the eagles' eyrie. The overhanging rock and nest in the crevice stood between me and the helicopter.

Even if they looked back at the cliff—which wasn't likely, because they were almost certainly scanning the ground for my movements—they still would see only the nest, and not me.

I had no flare, no way to signal them. I couldn't throw anything down to catch their attention. I couldn't even start an avalanche, because there weren't any loose rocks.

I watched helplessly as the helicopter sped off into the distance, searching the ground for me, not knowing that they'd passed within a hundred feet of me.

The helicopter made three large, sweeping turns across the valley, looking for signs of movement. But it did not return to the cliff face, and it did not come close enough for me to signal. They were gone a few minutes later. I listened miserably as the sound faded into the distance.

Perhaps they would return. But not for hours, or even days. They were almost certainly searching by grid, from a map, and they wouldn't return to this particular grid until they'd exhausted the other possibilities.

My heart sank. I was now, truly, on my own. There would be no rescue from the rangers. I'd have to get these eagles on my own. There was no other way.

△
CHAPTER 19

△ It was hard to shake the depression that had suddenly come crashing down around my ears. But I had to shake it. I *had* to! There was still work to be done, a lot of it. I had eagles to save. Now was no time to cry over the helicopter's flight.

I slipped the gloves on. They felt awkward and bulky, but it was the best protection I had. The eagles could be vicious. I just hoped the gloves were enough.

The eagles had suddenly grown very quiet. I think the helicopter scared them. The sound of the helicopter blades was so unusual out here, where the most they ever heard was the wind whipping through their lonely summit.

I decided to move quickly, seize the moment. They wouldn't be quiet for long. I had to take advantage of every opportunity.

I gripped the rope again with one hand and got ready

to fend the eagles off with the other. I rocked once, twice, a third time. Then I let loose with a terrible yell and pulled myself up with one ferocious yank that nearly ripped the pitons loose.

I was up! I reached out quickly with my free arm and pushed myself up entirely, the way I'd always gotten to the top of the tar-covered roof of my elementary school after someone had just booted the kickball onto it.

I'd been a champion roof-climber. I could climb up onto our elementary school roof from the top of the metal balcony that overlooked the school's back entrance faster than anyone else around. I just used one arm to push and shinnied up.

I did exactly that here. The only difference was that, instead of tar, I was now boosting myself up onto rock and grass.

I was vulnerable to attack for a moment, until I could get my second arm up and over the edge. But the eagles didn't attack, as I'd expected.

They were so startled by both the helicopter, and then me, that they had moved to the edge of the nest. Both of them.

For there were, in fact, two baby eagles. Only they didn't look like babies. They were bigger than any bird I'd ever come across—even now, when they were not yet fully grown.

One of them spread its wings and opened its beak very wide as I clambered up onto the edge of the eyrie. I was sure it was going to attack. But a tiny *scree!* came out instead. The other eagle, meanwhile, cowered behind the first.

Both eagles were perched on the opposite side of the eyrie, right at the brink. I thought, briefly, that maybe the best thing to do would be to just shove them out of the nest, forcing them to go out on their own.

But, just as quickly, I dismissed the thought. They'd just come right back after I'd left, and I would have gained nothing.

No, I had to do my best to capture one, or both, of them. It seemed impossible, to say the least.

The eagles were nearly as big as I was. Or at least they seemed that way, especially with their wings outstretched.

In fact, they were easily less than half my size. Full-grown eagles, I knew, rarely got bigger than three feet in length. And these weren't nearly full grown.

The bolder one spread its wings again. Its squeal was louder this time, and it cocked its head to one side. I could see it was preparing for a charge. In one moment, it would duck its head low and come at me. I had to do something.

In one blinding, dazzling moment, I knew what I had to do. It was my only hope. The entire plan sort of dropped down on me all at once.

I would wait for the bold eagle to charge. If I could dodge it, or fend it off, then I could reach across and grab the other eagle, the quieter one. I would have the element of surprise on my side that way. Plus, the bold one could not defend its sibling.

Of course, if the bold eagle was successful in its effort to push me from the nest, then I was in a *lot* of trouble! But I was certain I could take the eagle's charge.

Before my dad had died, he and I would wrestle a lot, usually on a big round rug in the living room. Mom hated it when we wrestled in the living room, but Dad usually just ignored her complaints.

Dad used to stand in the middle of the rug and lean way over, to draw my charge. Then, when I came racing at him, he'd suddenly shift his weight and I'd rush by just like some foolish bull charging at a red cape in the hands of an experienced matador.

I'd learned eventually not to fall for that dumb trick. I'd just barrel right into my dad. But the eagle had never wrestled my dad before, and I could try the same trick here.

I leaned over to the right and started shaking my head at the bold eagle, just to make sure it got the picture. It cocked its head, and its beak inched back a little farther, paused, and then the eagle charged.

In a flash, I shifted all of my weight to the left to avoid the onrush of wings, beak, and claws. I nearly tumbled right off the edge of the eyrie.

"AAAiiiggghhhiiiiieeee!" I screamed, clinging tenaciously to the cliff edge. The eagle brushed right by me, flapping its wings furiously. One claw caught my shirt, doing some damage. Its beak drove into my leg, but I ignored the pain.

I righted myself in a split second, and then countercharged. With the daypack trailing behind, I lunged across the eyrie. I'd never wrestled an eagle to the ground before, so I did what seemed the most logical— I tried to pin it down all at once and force it, head first, into the open daypack.

I grabbed the eagle and pulled it toward the center of the nest. The eagle put up a mighty fuss. It shrieked loudly and tried to pull its neck back so that it could go for my eyes. I squeezed harder and pulled it under me.

The bolder eagle, meanwhile, had turned and was now ready for a second charge. It lowered the boom, right smack in my backside. This time, I yelped with pain. The beak had come perilously close to doing major damage. It hurt like crazy.

But I still managed to ignore the bold one, concentrating all of my energy and efforts on the eagle that was now pinned beneath me. I slammed the daypack down in front of me. I'd have just one chance, and I had to make the best of it.

I let the eagle up slightly, drew the daypack in toward me, and pushed with everything I had. The eagle's head disappeared into the daypack. It squealed louder still, and I pushed even harder. I got its body inside, and I held the edges tight to keep it from escaping.

The second eagle thrashed around and around, trying to get out. But sensing that it was defeated, it stopped moving around almost as suddenly as it had begun. It went perfectly still.

Once, in our old house, my dad had taught me how to catch mice while they were still alive. He loved doing it. He thought it was a kick, kind of like a sport.

"Anybody can set a trap and kill mice," my dad would say. "But to catch them alive—now *that's* a trick."

My dad would set up a baby monitor in the kitchen pantry. Then he'd wait until late at night in the winter, after we'd gone upstairs, and listen to the monitor for the sounds of a mouse scrabbling around in the pantry.

My dad would creep down the stairs quietly and, before the mouse could react, open the door and slide this heavy piece of cardboard in front of the open door so the mouse could not escape. He'd turn the light on and start clearing the shelves.

The mouse was freaking, of course. It was running around on the shelves, trying to hide behind cans and boxes. But finally there would be no place left to hide. My dad had removed all of them to the other side of the cardboard.

The first time I watched him do this I was amazed. But when I saw him do it a second, third, and fourth time, I knew what to expect.

Once all the boxes and cans had been cleared away, the mouse would make a mad, frantic dash for the edge of the doorway and the cardboard, trying first to dig out and then trying to hop up over the cardboard. When this failed, as it always did, the mouse would run back and cower in the far corner.

Then, my dad would take this rectangular plastic container that was about two feet long and settle it down over the catatonic mouse. Once trapped inside the plastic container, the mouse would go crazy trying to escape. It would run around and around the edges, looking for a crack to escape under.

Finding none, it would finally settle down quietly in a corner and remain there for the rest of the time my dad and I watched it. It didn't move or budge, even when we tapped on the top of the container. It just stayed put, waiting for an opportunity to escape. Eventually my dad would take the mouse outside and let it loose.

That was what the eagle was doing. It had chosen—for a reason I couldn't possibly understand—not to struggle any further. It had been captured, and it would bide its time until it saw a chance to escape. I was able to zip the daypack up without any further trouble.

The bold eagle, though, was giving me fits. While I

was wrestling with its sibling, it had attacked my back, my neck, my legs, and just about every other exposed part of my anatomy. I would have welts there for days, I was sure.

I turned to face my attacker, the second eagle safely tucked inside. *"Aaaaggghhh!"* I yelled at it. "Go! Fly away! Leave me alone!"

The eagle didn't immediately retreat. It just flapped its wings and screeched at me.

"Get! Go, you! I mean it!" I yelled a second time, waving my arms as I yelled.

The eagle finally retreated slightly under my withering barrage of words. But it was not yet ready to leave the nest, so I gave it some extra encouragement. I pulled my hammer free and began to prod it, hard. I caught it twice before it got the picture. It fled—half tumbling, half flying—from the nest.

I watched it fall down the mountain for close to twenty feet or so before it got its wings flapping. It made a slow arc down and then, finally, leveled off and began to rise again. I breathed a sigh of relief.

"See ya," I called out to it. "Don't come back." I watched it catch a wind current and lift steadily upward, until it had risen above the eyrie and disappeared to the east.

I lifted the daypack onto my back gingerly and strapped it into place. The eagle did not struggle. It was resting like a heavy stone in the pack. But I knew that at any moment it could spring to life, so I fastened the cinch on the pack as hard as I could.

The next part would not be easy, but I couldn't see how it could possibly be any harder than what I'd just been through. In fact, I didn't think I'd ever find anything as difficult in my entire life.

"Come on, eagle," I said to the still life inside my pack. "It's time to go home."

The eagle didn't answer. I only hoped it would remain quiet. That was the only way I would ever get it to safety.

△

CHAPTER 20

△ Surprisingly, the trip down was quick and uneventful. It was a whole lot easier than the trip up. I climbed down hand over hand, leaving the rope and pitons in place. I didn't climb down rapidly, because the eagle on my back was too heavy. But I was still able to make the entire trip in less than an hour.

I didn't know exactly where I was, of course, once I got to the bottom. I had no food except for the four jerky strips I was still saving for the eagle. I had no water, and only a compass to guide me.

It would be brutal trying to carry the eagle as well as my own pack. I would be carrying close to thirty pounds, I figured, which was heavier than anything I'd ever carried. I had no idea if I could make it.

But I had to try. I had to get far enough away from the cliff and the eyrie so that the eagle I was carrying would think twice before it returned there. I wanted to give it at least a chance of survival.

I hoped that if we could get far away, the eagle would try to hunt on its own. If it did that often enough, then it could return to the eyrie: Once it had hunted without its parents, I thought it would be able to make it on its own.

I packed up and then placed the daypack with my little bundle of life on top. The eagle still hadn't moved. It was waiting for that one opening before it made its move.

There was no sign of its sibling high in the sky. The bold one had vanished, for the time being. My heart sank at the thought that maybe it had returned to the eyrie and was now sitting there, mewing or squealing softly, waiting for both its parents and its lost sibling to return.

But maybe not. There was no way of knowing. I would simply have to hope for the best.

I decided just to plunge straight down the mountain. With the heavy load and nothing to guide me—and no easy path through the forest to follow—it would take me at least two days to make my way through the sub-alpine region to the Kaweah River valley.

From the river, I could find my way home, I was certain of that. If worse came to worst, I could follow the river until I came to somebody, anybody, who could lead me to safety.

My first priority, though, was finding something to eat and drink. I was ready to drop from exhaustion.

The nearest stream was well down the mountain. I looked around. What to do?

I must have stared at the solution for several minutes before it finally dawned on me. The snow! Well, of course. How could I have been so dense?

I grabbed my hammer and rushed over to the base of the cliff, where most of the snow was packed. I knew the base of the snow mound was ice, and would be impossible to get to. But the top, once I'd scraped away the dirty upper layer, would be all right.

I got down on my hands and knees. I was so weak from the lack of sleep and nutrition that my eyes were blurry, but I swung the claw end of the hammer viciously, chipping away at the hard snow. White flecks of snow sprayed in all directions.

I dug a small hole before I laid the hammer to one side and reached with my hand. I scooped up some and put it in my mouth. It tasted awful. But it was water, or it would be eventually when it melted.

I stayed there for the longest time, scooping up handfuls of snow I was able to chip out. It wasn't quite the same as a cool mountain stream. But it was water, which I desperately had to have right now.

I thought about trying to save some for the eagle, but then thought better of it. There was no way to give the eagle any without risking the possibility that it would fly away. And I couldn't exactly store it in anything, or carry it with me.

I ate the snow until my hands were numb and raw, and my belly was as full as I could manage. Now, for something to eat.

That would not be easy. I'd have to go down some, to where there were trees. And even then, I had no idea what I could possibly find.

I thought about searching for berries. But they'd be hard to find by this time of year. The animals had eaten most of them. What did that leave, then? Roots? I had no idea how to find them, or what to look for.

I almost laughed. Miss Lily was right. You had to study the *entire* forest, all of nature. You couldn't just pay attention to God's creatures. You had to look at *all* of His creation to understand.

OK, OK, I could see that. But what good did it do to understand that out here now? *Not much*, I thought glumly.

I eased into my pack. I'd just have to think of something as I walked. Like there was something I could think of.

I picked my way through the boulders and rocks gingerly. It was nearly impossible to walk. The pack was breaking my back. I felt like a badly broken-down mule. I'd never make it to the lowlands.

I had to lean forward a little as I walked. If I tried to walk straight, and my foot slipped or skidded on a rock, then I went lurching backward. I did that once, and it was more than enough to teach me a lesson.

The only problem with leaning forward, of course, was that when I hit a steep part, it was nearly impossible to keep from just barreling straight down the mountain. At those parts, I just sort of skidded down the rocks.

About fifteen minutes down the mountain, the bold eagle sibling returned—with a vengeance. I never even saw it coming. It gave no squeal or cry of warning. It just dive-bombed straight at me.

I only caught it coming at me full tilt at the last minute. Fortunately, it came at me from the front, not the rear. Otherwise, I would not have had a prayer.

It came hurtling down from the sky, almost at a vertical drop, until it was about a hundred feet from me. Then, it leveled off and came racing straight at my face. It flapped its wings once, twice, a third time. Then it was on me.

I ducked at the last second and fell to my knees as the eagle went racing by, missing me by just a few inches. I could feel the warm blast of the feathers as it swept by.

There had been no time even to yell. A cold chill swept through my body an instant later as I realized how close I'd come to taking a beak directly in the face.

Still on my knees, I turned and watched the eagle begin to climb skyward again for a round trip and a second try. It most definitely did *not* like the fact that I had taken its sibling from the nest. Not at all.

I grinned viciously. Well, good. That was a start. It was fighting for something, now. It wasn't just pining away in the eyrie, waiting for parents that would never return.

Now, all I had to do was keep the young eagle from killing me and we all might have a chance at surviving this thing.

I also realized immediately that I had to keep the eagle in my pack with me for as long as I could. For, I knew, the eagle now climbing toward the heavens would not rest until its sibling was free.

And that was a good thing. It meant that it would not remain in the nest. It would remain free, away from the eyrie. And the more time it spent on its own —even if it was only hunting me and not real prey— the better were its chances of surviving on its own.

I looked around frantically for anything that could serve as cover. I was still a good fifty yards from the treeline. I started to stumble toward it. I would never get there before the eagle tried a second time. So I kept one eye on the ground in front of me, and one eye on the sky.

I was ready for the eagle's charge the second time, though, and it wasn't as hard to get away. The young eagle was all might and muscle, with very little finesse. It came charging straight at me. I ducked again, at the last second, and it went hurtling past me harmlessly.

It got a third crack at me before I got to the treeline. But I escaped unharmed. I began to breathe more easily once I'd reached the relative safety of the short pines.

The young eagle circled above, uncertain what to do next. I could almost see it thinking, looking, waiting for a chance to drop down into a clearing for a fourth shot at me.

But I wasn't about to give it that chance. I walked from tree trunk to tree trunk, hurrying through openings and avoiding anything that even remotely looked like a meadow. That eagle wouldn't charge me again, not if I could help it.

Finally, the eagle must have sensed that it would not get another chance, because it settled into a routine as well. It would circle overhead for quite a long time, then settle down on the highest limb of the tallest tree it could find, and watch.

After it had done this several times, I stopped watching it. I just kept to the trees and began to consider how I was going to find something to eat in this barren landscape.

Actually, of course, it wasn't barren. There were trees and pine cones and grass and shrubs and plants and flowers and all kinds of things. Which was just great—if you were a deer and liked to munch on stuff like that.

None of this did me even the slightest bit of good. I had to have something with nutrition to it, something that was good for me. I needed, well . . . I didn't know what I needed, but plants and flowers didn't cut it.

I started to go over in my mind what each of the creatures I knew actually ate. Bears, I knew, went after berries and roots, mostly. But there wouldn't be any berries up here at this time of year. So that was hopeless. And even if I found some, I had no way of knowing if they were poisonous or not, or even if they were good for me. And roots? Not a chance. I didn't even know where to begin.

Deer went after grass and shoots on trees. So did most of the other animals I could think of. It was a lost cause. I wasn't going to find anything.

I walked along slowly. I was so tired I just wanted to break down and stop, right in the middle of the woods at 10,000 feet or however high up we were. I didn't care. I just wanted to stop and go to sleep.

It finally occurred to me that maybe that wasn't such a bad idea. I was exhausted. I desperately needed sleep. I'd gotten almost none in that sling on the mountainside. I needed food, it was true. But I also needed sleep nearly as badly.

I decided, finally, to find a place I could rest for a couple of hours. But what would I do with the eagle in my daypack? And what about the eagle overhead?

I had to risk it. There was no other choice. I couldn't keep stumbling along. I had to rest.

After a few minutes of looking, I spotted a stand of trees that would serve my purpose. I would make my camp there. I'd already decided what I was going to do with the eagle in my pack.

Once I was settled, I pulled my climbing rope free and made a loop at the end that I could slip over one of the eagle's claws and tighten. Then I tied the other end of the rope to the base of a tree, so that it would have enough rope to hop around but not enough, really, to get airborne.

I had no idea if this would work. But I couldn't just keep the eagle stuffed inside my pack forever. I couldn't feed it that way, anyway.

I pulled the daypack off my large pack gently. I didn't want to get the eagle riled up right now. I felt the pack to see how the eagle had settled. I was in luck. Its claws were down at the bottom, near the zipper.

I carefully worked the zipper open with the hand that held the looped rope. I inched it open ever so slightly.

The eagle suddenly started to thrash around for all it was worth. It had spotted its opening, and it went for it with all of the strength it could muster. It pecked and thrashed and flapped with all it had.

One claw slipped free of the pack, though, and I jammed the rope on as fast as I could. I cinched it tight quickly, and then stepped back. The eagle thrashed around a little while longer, and then rested. At that point, I reached over and unzipped the pack entirely.

The eagle poked its head out and stared at me balefully. It mewed once, ominously, and then tried to lift off from the ground. The rope, however, held to the base of the tree and the eagle came fluttering back to the earth.

The eagle tried over and over to lift off, never with

146

any success. Eventually, it gave up. Finally realizing that the rope had it tethered to the earth, it folded up its wings.

I felt bad for the eagle. But I felt even worse for myself. I was starving, weak, and near collapse by now. I had to have something to eat soon, or I would be in big trouble.

I leaned up against the base of a tree and rested my head. Oh, how I wished that helicopter would come roaring over the hill now! I'd give anything to go home. I didn't care if I was grounded for life. I just wanted to go home.

The sharp *click-click* nearby startled me. It was a strange sound, one I hadn't heard before. I looked up. The sound had come from the rocks above me.

An absolutely huge bighorn ram had wandered into a meadow nearby. It was that time of year, when the first snows of the coming fall drive the sheep from the highest alpine meadows to slopes where the wind keeps the ground clear for foraging.

It was also the time of year when the males try to kill each other to "win" the ewes. I heard a second set of hooves come *click-clicking* across the stones.

As if we weren't even there, the two bighorn sheep squared off. They were huge, maybe close to six feet. They had enormous coiled horns and short dark brown hair all around except for tan patches on top.

Both sheep lowered their heads and came hurtling at each other. *Crack!* The sound echoed for half a mile in either direction. It was especially loud from my front-row seat.

I felt strangely comforted watching this ancient ritual. It was almost as if God were telling me that everything would be all right. Nature had its own rhythm. I

147

had not upset that balance. I was part of it, and everything would work out in its own time.

The two rams butted heads for close to half an hour, with neither one giving an inch and neither winning the match. They eventually retreated to neutral corners, to try some other time.

I knew this kind of fighting would go on for a good part of the fall, until it was clear who was the stronger of the rams. In the spring, when the herds were in the high country, a single lamb would be born on a narrow, protected ledge.

The sheep chose those ledges to protect the young lambs. But even there, I knew, eagles or cougars could get to them. The first moments of that young lamb's life were the most dangerous, so the ewes were smart. They went to the most precarious part of the landscape to shelter themselves from predators.

The natural quiet of the land returned after the bighorn sheep had moved on. The eagle had settled down to wait. I knew it was biding its time.

I decided to see if it would eat some of the jerky I'd saved. I had no idea whether it would take it, but I had to try. I fumbled around in my pack until I found them.

I stared at the jerky for the longest time. There were four pieces. Surely, I could eat one or two of the strips, and feed the rest to the eagle. What harm would it do?

"No!" I said loudly. "I won't. This is for the eagle."

Before I could think about it further, I marched over to a spot just outside the eagle's range. It didn't move. It eyed me warily.

I sat down and considered how best to get this job done. In the end, I decided that I had no choice. I tossed the jerky strip as close to the eagle as I could manage. It was a decent toss. The strip fell about two feet in front of the eagle.

The eagle looked from me to the strip, back to me, then back to the strip. Finally, it flapped its wings a couple of times and ambled over to it. I knew it had to be as hungry as I was. It hesitated only for a moment, then reached down and snatched it up. The strip was gone shortly.

I tossed the remaining pieces to the eagle. By the fourth strip, the eagle was waiting for the meal. It followed the toss of my hand, and nearly grabbed the meat from the air on its way down. It even mewed for some more.

"Sorry, buddy, that's all," I said, holding both hands out to show it I didn't have any more.

I settled back against the tree again. I didn't move for a long time. I was too stiff and tired to budge.

I looked up at the sound of chattering high above in a nearby tree. A Western gray squirrel, which you rarely saw except out in the wild like this, poked its head around a tree limb and looked down at me.

It scampered down the tree, chattering the entire way. When it got to the ground, I could see that it had something in its mouth. I grinned ruefully. It was an acorn, which the dumb squirrel could eat and survive on.

I sat up straight. Wait a minute. Something Miss Lily had once told me came tumbling down through the mist of my brain. Acorns. Something about acorns. But what was it?

"Hey, squirrel, what's the deal with that acorn, anyway?" I called out. The squirrel stared at me for a moment, then disappeared around another tree and climbed up to safety. But the idea had been planted. I remembered now.

I searched around inside my pack frantically. I needed my flint and steel. Then I'd need some twigs and sticks for a fire, a flat stone and another stone to grind with. And then I would need some acorns. Lots of them.

△
CHAPTER 21

△ It took me nearly an hour to gather up enough acorns. I gathered them in my pockets, carried them back to my little camp, and dropped them into the pile I was building. I had no idea how many I'd need. I just found as many as I could.

Then, it took me a while to pry the acorns loose from their little "caps" that held them to the trees. Fortunately, many of them were already free, or the caps came off easily.

I was ready to try grinding them up. I wasn't exactly sure what the best method was, so I just put one of them between the two stones I'd managed to find. I pressed down hard. The acorn squirted out and skittered across the ground.

"Hey!" I yelled after the fleeing acorn. "Get back here!"

I got the hang of it on the third acorn. The trick was to place the acorn in a rounded hollow of the stone on the ground and then grind down with the stone on top. I quickly abandoned the initial grinding stone I'd found and searched until I'd discovered a much sharper stone to grind with.

As soon as I'd ground the acorn into a coarse, powdery dust, I swept it onto the tarp I'd laid out beside my little work area.

It was hard work, and slow going. But after a while, I'd built up a good little pile on the tarp. I rested for a few minutes, and then attacked the rest of the acorns I'd gathered.

When I was finished, I was thoroughly exhausted. But now was the hard part. Miss Lily said that acorns had something called tannic acid that had to be leached from the acorn meal.

The way the Indians did it, she'd told me, was to put the acorn meal on a big cloth and then run boiling water through the cloth over and over until all the tannic acid had been leached out. Then the acorn meal was dried out, and they did all sorts of stuff with it after that.

Obviously, I couldn't do that here. So I had to improvise. I had an old battered tin cup I always hiked with so that I could scoop up mountain spring water. I pulled it free and then went off in search of a natural spring. There had to be one nearby. There almost always was at this level.

I followed the greenery. That was always a sure sign of water. The greener the landscape, the more likely a source of water was nearby. I struck pay dirt almost immediately. A little spring was about a hundred yards from where I'd settled. There was a small trickle of water coming out of it, and it didn't take long to fill my cup.

I carried the water back to camp carefully. I would need every drop. Once there, I set the water down and began to gather twigs. It was against the law to build a fire out here, but I had no choice. I had to eat, and this was the only thing I could think of.

I piled the twigs, small ones, on the ground. I wasn't an expert with the flint and steel in my pack—Ashley was actually pretty good with it and nearly always got fires started before I did—but I got one going eventually. I blew on it gently until it was going well.

I let the fire burn down just a little, then I placed the precious tin cup in a low part. I waited anxiously while the water boiled. Once I could see the bubbles start to rise in the water, I took the extra shirt from my pack and carefully twisted enough of the acorn "dust" into a corner of the shirt so that it would fit inside the tin cup.

Once the water was boiling, I dunked the acorn meal into the water. I had no idea how long it would take to leach the tannic acid, so I just held it there for a while and then pulled it free. I dumped the soaked meal on the tarp, in a new pile, quickly piled more dry meal into the shirt and repeated the process.

When too much of the water had either evaporated or spilled from the little tin cup, I emptied it out and ran back to the spring and got more. Then I started the whole thing all over again.

The sun was starting to set to the west again by the time I'd finished, but I no longer cared. I had food. Or, at least, I *thought* I had food. It looked like wet mush, but it was food. It would fill my stomach.

"Your dinner was better'n mine," I called over to the eagle, which had watched my adventure with a quite curious eye. The eagle had definitely perked up quite a lot since its own meal.

I had no idea what to do with acorn mush now that I'd actually finished it. I couldn't make pancakes or use it with bread or anything like that.

I closed my eyes and just dug in. I shoveled the stuff into my mouth and swallowed. It had a bitter, acrid taste. It was a little like eating bark. But it was absolutely, gloriously, incredibly wonderful. I ate every last drop, and wished I had more.

There was still a huge hole in my stomach. I wanted more to eat, but this would do. I'd make it until tomorrow, which was the goal, after all.

I decided to make camp where I was. There was no use trying to find a better place. Not now. There was only an hour or so of light left, and I had no clue where I was, anyway. Better to wait until morning and make one final push to find the Kaweah River.

I said a silent "thank you" to God. Out here, it didn't seem strange. It seemed perfectly natural and fine. I felt like I could hear His voice quite clearly—more clearly than I ever had before in my life.

There was still my mother and stepfather to face. There would be an awful price to pay for what I'd done. But I was prepared to face it now.

As I lay down to sleep that night, for the longest time I watched the stars come out. The eagle was quiet. It had really settled down. It no longer moved around anxiously.

Its sibling had been gone for hours. It had gone somewhere, I wasn't sure where. I hoped it had gone to hunt, but perhaps I would never know.

I closed my eyes finally. Sleep came swiftly. I welcomed it like a long lost friend.

△
CHAPTER 22

△ The cry of the eagle woke me. It was a cry of welcome, not of anger. I rolled free of my sleeping bag and opened a weary eye.

The sun had not yet risen over the ridge to the east, but it was still quite light outside, enough to see by.

I glanced up just in time to see the eagle make its landing. It was the sibling. And it was carrying something.

I almost burst into tears at the sight. The eagle had, indeed, been out hunting. In its mouth was a limp, freshly killed rabbit. The eagle had hunted on its own!

The eagle kind of half-waddled over to its sibling. It laid the rabbit down on the ground between them, and they began to eat voraciously. I watched in pure joy. Every nerve was screaming with delight at the scene I was now watching.

I knew, now, that the eagles would make it. Or at least they had a fighting chance, once the rangers had either arrested or driven the hunters away from the other side of Cascade Mountain.

The eagle I'd carried with me down the mountain looked at me briefly before joining in with its sibling. Almost as if to say thanks. I smiled. "Go to it," I called out. "It's all yours."

I had no desire whatsoever to join in. The rabbit was theirs. Even if there was some way to cook it, I didn't think I could bring myself to do so. I was as hungry this morning as I'd been the day before, but even the gnawing pangs of hunger didn't make that rabbit seem appealing.

When the eagles had finished their meal, the sibling began to peck at the rope that held the other tethered to the earth. Both of them started to work at the rope.

It dawned on me that my work was now finished. I had to free the eagle. Keeping it here any longer was foolish. There was no need to take it farther. I was almost certain that both would be just fine now, even if they returned to the eyrie.

I pulled the tarp down and approached the two eagles. "Watch out!" I yelled. "Comin' in!" I didn't want to frighten either one of them, but I had to get close in order to throw the tarp over the tethered eagle.

The bold eagle squealed at me once, but then took off. It landed on a lower limb nearby and watched. It was ready to attack at any minute. I could see that quite clearly.

I moved quickly. The captured eagle flapped only once as I drew near and then threw the tarp over. It went crazy once the tarp was over it, but I subdued it quickly.

I glanced over my shoulder. The other eagle was about to come at me, so I only had a few seconds. I pinned the eagle beneath me to the ground and ran my hand along the rope until I got to the claw. Feeling around in the dark, I pulled on one end of the loop hard until it came free. Then I yanked it over the eagle's claw, grabbed a corner of the tarp, and stepped back.

The eagle almost didn't know how to react at first. It hopped a couple of times, tested its wings once, and stared at me for a little while. But once it was satisfied that everything was in working order, it lifted off the ground and joined its sibling in the air.

I watched for the longest time as the two of them caught the air currents and glided well up into the sky, side by side, and finally disappeared over a nearby peak. It was a sight I would never forget.

I packed up camp and headed down the mountain. I was cold, but not nearly as cold as I'd been up on the mountain. There were no clouds in the sky, so I figured it would be a nice warm day eventually.

I wandered down the mountain for a long time without paying a whole lot of attention to where I was going. I had no landmarks to go by. I just knew I had to go down, a long way.

I almost stumbled right into the elk. I'd come to a clearing, one of the few real meadows to be found anywhere on the side of the mountain. I'd wandered out into it, almost out of curiosity.

The elk, which spends the summer in the alpine meadows, was probably on its way down to the lowlands and had paused here to eat. I almost walked right into it. The thing was huge, maybe eight or nine feet long, with eight points on its antlers.

The two of us stared at each other for several long moments, then the elk went back to eating. I was not a threat. I watched it eat for a while, and then moved on. I crossed right through the center of the meadow.

I was so numb with fatigue, pain, and hunger that I didn't notice the predator's tracks until it was almost too late. I got to the edge of the woods and looked down. I stopped and stared hard at the tracks at the edge of the clearing. They were fresh, and unmistakable.

A wolverine! Here, in this meadow. I figured the tracks had just been made, probably that morning. The marks from the distinctive pads and five-toed claws were still moist in the soft ground. They were similar to a small bear's tracks, but I was certain they belonged to a wolverine.

Which meant the wolverine could be quite close by. It was probably waiting for the elk to get closer to the treeline, where it could attack without having to run much. The elk was smart. It was grazing nearly in the center of the meadow, where it could either run or attack with its sharp antlers.

Wolverines rarely went after a healthy elk, so I quickly figured that the elk out in this meadow had to be sick. That was probably why it was out here alone, not with a herd. Most likely, the wolverine had been stalking it for some time.

I ran back out into the meadow. I yelled at the elk at the top of my lungs. The elk, startled, looked up and then started to run in the opposite direction.

The wolverine came charging out at both of us an instant later. The wolverine was small compared to the elk, maybe a third its size. It was stocky, with short legs. It loped out to meet both of us.

For better or worse, I was now in the middle—and

part of the hunt. I ran toward the wolverine, trying to head it off before it got the elk.

The elk started one way, then went another. Finally, it turned on its heels and ran back, past me. The wolverine came loping at us, then stopped a few feet short of me and bared its teeth, which were considerable.

The wolverine didn't know what to make of me. Was I a predator or a nuisance? It hesitated long enough, though, for the elk to escape out the other side of the meadow and into the trees. We both listened as it crashed through the underbrush.

Furious that I had chased away its meal, the wolverine bared its teeth a second time and prepared to charge me. I was now the prey, and I had no idea what to do. I pulled my pack free and held it out in front of me as a shield.

The familiar cry of the eagle reached my ears like a sweet melody. I glanced up once, quickly, just in time to see the eagle come hurtling down from the sky like a bolt out of heaven.

The eagle came screaming straight at the wolverine, and didn't begin to work its wings backward until it was quite close.

As the eagle drew close, the wolverine hissed and bared its teeth again. It snapped at the eagle as the two joined in combat. The eagle sunk its claws into the wolverine's furry hide and tried to lift it off the ground. The wolverine went crazy, rolling in every direction at once. The eagle dropped the wolverine to the ground and began to lift off again.

But the wolverine had seen more than enough. First me, and now the eagle. What was the deal, anyway?

All it wanted was a simple meal, and then we come along.

The wolverine turned and loped away into the trees. I started to breathe again as I watched its steady, tireless gait. I hoped I never saw a wolverine again—unless I was better prepared. They were terrifying creatures.

I looked up at the sky. The eagle soared higher. It joined a second eagle circling up where the wind currents carried it easily. I waved at them.

I had no idea why the eagle had come down to attack the wolverine. But I remembered the legend Miss Lily had told me, that when an eagle befriends you, it does so for life, and that you can always count on it in a time of trouble.

The eagle had come to my side in a time of trouble. So did I have a friend? I didn't know. Perhaps I would never see the eagle again, except on clear afternoons when it circled high above Cascade Mountain. Only time would tell.

I walked down the mountain again and considered all that I'd been through in the past few days. I'd changed. My life had been turned upside down. I was a different person now. Much, much different.

I heard the helicopter blades from a long way off. I fought the tears and ran out into an opening where they could see me. I waved for all I was worth.

They'd been searching for me for nearly two days. While the other kids were starting school, the rangers had been out looking for me.

I knew Mom would be out of her mind by now with fear. But it would be all right soon. Everything would be all right. I would be home, and safe.

Mark came tumbling out of the side door of the helicopter almost the moment it touched down. He ducked under the whirring blades and ran across the ground, nearly knocking me over with his big bear-hug embrace.

I held him tight. I was never more glad to see any-one than I was to see him. We didn't say anything for the longest time. We just held each other.

"I was so worried," Mark whispered, his voice cracking from the pain and emotion he'd felt. "But I knew you could take care of yourself. I just knew you could."

"I'm so tired," I answered at last, the tears coming freely. I leaned on him. Mark held me up. "I just wanna go home. Can we, please . . . Dad?"

About the Author

Jeff Nesbit is the author of many books for children and teenagers, including *A War of Words*, *The Sioux Society*, and *The Great Nothing Strikes Back*. He lives with his wife and their three children in Virginia.